THE ENFORCER

MAYHEM MAKERS

ZEPHYR HILLS PHANTOMS MC
BOOK ONE

DARLENE TALLMAN

CONTENTS

The ENFORCER

INTERNATIONAL BESTSELLING AUTHOR
DARLENE TALLMAN

COPYRIGHT

COVER MODEL: DYLAN HORSCH
PHOTOGRAPHER: FURIOUSFOTOG/GOLDEN CZERMAK
EDITORS: MARY KERN, MELANIE GRAY, NICOLE MCVEY, JENNIFER CORBIN, STEPHANIE ELLIS, BETH DILORETO, JENI CLANCY, SYLVIE HOWICK
PROOFERS: CHERYL HULLETT, NICOLE LLOYD, NICOLE MCVEY
FORMATTER: LIBERTY PARKER
COVER BY CLARISSE TAN OF CT COVER CREATIONS

DISCLAIMER / AUTHOR'S NOTE

MOTORCYCLES, MOBSTERS, AND MAYHEM AUTHOR EVENT proudly presents *The Mayhem Makers Series,* novels brought to you by several bestselling authors specializing in writing twisted chaos. You'll get all the bikers, mobsters, and dark romance your heart can handle.

The Mayhem Makers Series is a collection of works of fiction that mention the author signing **MOTORCYCLES, MOBSTERS, AND MAYHEM AUTHOR EVENT** *in each novel. No authors, assistants, models, or readers attending the event were harmed in the writing of these fictional works. Events mentioned are fictional additions to each author's novel and do not reflect what actually goes on at the aforementioned signing.*

The Enforcer is a shifter MC; there may be situations, language, and adult content that may make you uncomfortable. It is intended for mature audiences and as such, recommended for ages 18+ for the above-captioned reasons.

ACKNOWLEDGMENTS

What happens when an event organizer comes up with a wild plan to do a collaborative world? You get the Mayhem Makers and let me tell you, whatever your poison is with regard to bad boys, be it MC, mafia, mobster, or men focused on mayhem, you have Sapphire Knight to thank!

So, thank you, Sapphire, for putting this phenomenal signing together and also for thinking of such a unique idea to celebrate. I know I had a blast writing this first book, especially featuring author friends!

XOXOXO

Darlene

DEDICATION

For my readers who asked for a shifter MC. I hope you enjoy the guys from Zephyr Hills! As always, it's a fictitious place (kind of; I'm sure there's a town out there with the same name), and because the bulk of this first book surrounded the MMM 2023 signing, I didn't go into a lot of detail. Thankfully, my muses decided there'll be more than the three books I originally planned, so you'll become very familiar with the gorgeous place I see in my mind's eye.

XOXOXO

Dar

BLURB

Tressa Powers hasn't had an easy life. She's learned to keep to herself. Growing up, books were her escape. When she finally purchased an e-reader, she found a whole new world — indie authors. Tressa gets the chance to attend a book signing where many of her favorite authors will be. Real-life bikers will also be in attendance. She decides to splurge on a VIP ticket to the event instead of a general admission one since it will come with a swag bag.

While traveling to the hotel she'll be staying at, she gets a flat tire. A tall, tattooed biker stops to help her change the tire. Even though she doesn't get a good look at the man, she feels a sense of longing. Something she's never experienced before. Pushing the sensation aside, she vows to enjoy her once-in-lifetime dream. Tressa doesn't expect to see him again or be in a position so many of her favorite heroines find themselves in.

Enroute to the clubhouse, Chaos spots a vehicle on the side of the road. From what he can see, it's a female trying to change the tire. His mother's teachings return to him causing him to stop and offer her help. Because of the gear he wears while riding, Chaos isn't able to catch her scent. Once he's finished helping her, he continues on his way. At the clubhouse, he's told the club was invited to a book signing so the attendees can get a taste of what a real biker looks like. Zephyr Hills Phantoms MC are shifters; something that's a well-kept secret among the humans. Regardless, he's one of the members who is attending. While walking through the venue, he catches a whiff of something positively delicious. Following the scent of lilac, he comes across the woman he helped earlier. His wolf clearly says, "Mate."

When he watches a horrible club, the Bastions MC, corral his mate into a nondescript van, everyone in the vicinity will find out how he got his road name because he goes berserk.

Suitable for ages 18+ due to adult themes, language, and situations

CHARACTER LIST

Fox - President
Sly - VP
Chaos - Enforcer
Stealth - SAA
Popeye - Secretary/IT
Ledger - Treasurer
Ogre - Road Captain
Lobo - Patch
Bolt - Patch
Attila - Patch
Prospect
Prospect
Teeny - club girl
Becca - club girl

RENDA - CLUB GIRL

AND, OF COURSE, ANY AUTHOR FRIENDS WHOSE

NAMES SHOW UP IN THIS BOOK!

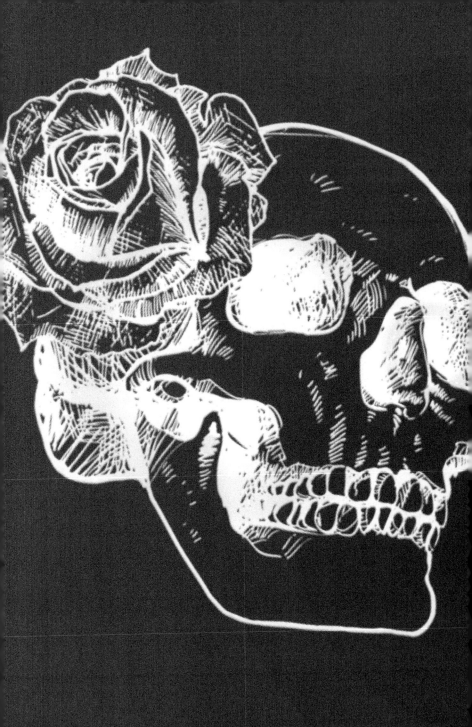

PROLOGUE

"Tressa, you're always in the way," my stepmother yelled.

"I'm sorry, Nancy," I replied as I hurried to grab my homework and stuff it in my backpack.

"Once you've cleaned up your mess, get the table set. Your father is bringing home guests tonight, so you'll eat in your room."

"Yes, ma'am," I said. Putting my backpack in my room, I came back out, washed my hands, then took the plates she had on the counter and carefully set the table. The last time I did it wrong, she slapped my hands with a wooden spoon, so I'm trying my best to make sure everything is just right. She does that a lot, though, especially when my daddy isn't around. He never sees the bruises or marks she leaves behind, and I'm afraid to tell him what happens when he's away from home because I don't want him to be sad. As I place the silverware on the cloth napkins she laid out for me, I wonder again why I can't live with my aunt. She's my mother's sister and I know she loves me, unlike the woman my dad married less than a year after my mom died.

After the table is set, complete with glasses for water and candles in the middle, I head to the kitchen and grab the bowl of macaroni and cheese sitting on the counter for me, then go to my room, grateful that I went to the library today and got two new books. With my homework done, at least I'll have something to do before it's time to go to bed. Not that anyone will check on me tonight since they're having guests. It'll be up to me to take a bath and make sure I have everything laid out for school tomorrow. But that's nothing unusual for me these days. I'm just happy I can escape, even if only for a little while, in the land of make believe.

———

"TRESSA, NOW THAT YOU'RE EIGHTEEN, IT'S TIME YOU got out on your own," Nancy stated, standing over me with her hands on her hips. "You've got a job so it shouldn't be difficult to find your own place."

I looked at her in horror. "Where am I going to find some-place to live with what I make?" I worked at the local book-store, and while the money was good enough to ensure I could buy the clothes and things I needed, there was no way I'd be able to afford to live on my own. I also wondered if my father agreed with her, although I suspected he didn't have a clue. It was all likely her idea, and she would present it to him as though *I* decided to move out. Of course, living under her roof had been hell, so even though this was going to be difficult for me, I'd figure it out so I could finally get peace in my life.

"I'm sure you'll come up with something," she replied, her lip curled in disdain. "You've been a drain on the house long enough, don't you think?"

I don't bother answering her. Instead, I stand and head to my room to see if I can find someplace else to live. Surely someone will have a room to rent, right?

———

"TRESSA, I THINK YOU SHOULD GO," MY FRIEND AND roommate, Nicole, said. "You've been designing covers for a lot of the authors who will be there, plus you proofread as well. Why not go and meet them? This signing is going to be huge, and with it being called MMM, you know you'll be able to get all the pretties we both like to read!"

"I don't know, Nini. I mean, you know how shy I am."

"Which is exactly why you should do it!" she exclaimed. "When will you get another chance to do something like this?"

I really lucked out when I answered Nicole's ad for a female roommate. Despite my shyness, we quickly became friends, and it was her encouragement that had me taking a graphic design course at the local college. Shortly after, I found the indie community, and not too long ago, I began designing covers for some of the authors I had read.

Ah, the worlds I've lived in through my books. Strong, handsome, capable men who loved and cherished their women. While I loved everything I read, my favorites were the motorcycle club romances. Seeing that so many of my favorite authors were going to be at MMM in Lake Conroe, Texas, I decided to live a little and buy myself a ticket.

"Do you want to come with me?" I asked.

"Girl, you know I'd love to, but I can't get the time off of work. But I can get you set up in a hotel nearby using my friends and family discount to help you save some money."

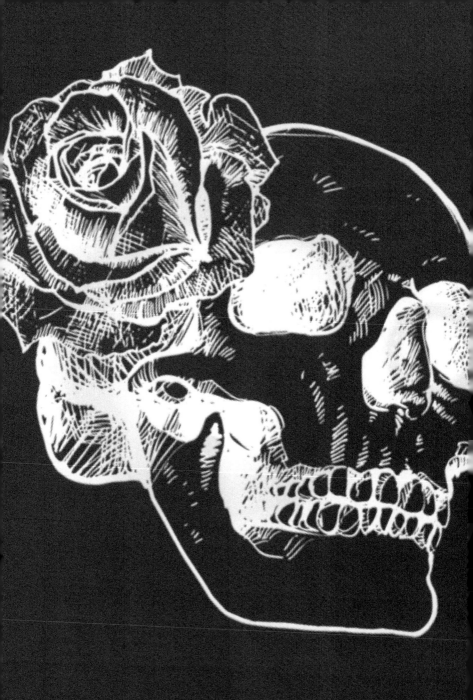

CHAPTER ONE

TRESSA

"Dang it all, Ruby!" I exclaim, kicking the flat tire. "Why you gotta do me like this?" My Jeep Renegade, Ruby, doesn't answer as I begin the process of taking out the spare tire from the trunk then getting the X socket I need to remove the lug nuts. Thank God my dad showed me how to change a tire because so far, despite sitting alongside I-30 for thirty minutes, not one person has slowed or even stopped to offer any help. It was one of the few things he taught me because my stepmonster didn't really like it when we spent time together, but he insisted, since as he told her, I needed to know how to do the basics in case there was no one around to help me.

Rolling up the sleeves of my hoodie, I make short work of jacking the back of my car up, being sure that I've put a chock block behind the front wheel, so Ruby doesn't roll. The first few lug nuts come off without any issue, but the last one seems to be holding on for dear life.

"This isn't going to work," I grunt out, putting all my strength into trying to turn the tool so I can loosen the damn thing. "Come on, you're killing my vibe right now. I want to get there so I can settle in and make sure I've got my plan of attack mapped out and ready for tomorrow."

True to her word, Nicole got me set up at a hotel not far from the event venue, and even though I won't be at the fancy resort itself, a lot of other readers, as well as some authors themselves, are also booked at the same hotel as I am from what she was able to see. I took advantage of preorder specials from some of my favorite authors as well, getting signing-only add-ons to my orders, then somehow, I got approved for a credit card with a five-hundred-dollar limit on it so I can hopefully buy some more. While Nicole pre ordered some as well, my plan is to surprise her by getting her some of her favorites as a 'just because' kind of thing.

The two of us spent hours creating some unique gifts for the authors I've done covers for, along with smaller bags for those I've proofread, and I'm excited to pass them out tomorrow. I also bought a cart to haul my stuff around, although I suspect I'll be making trips out to Ruby to unload what I've gotten so I have room for more books. We even put together two bookshelves which are waiting in my room for all the pretties I anticipate getting this weekend. I love the place we rent; both of our rooms are master bedrooms with their own attached bathrooms, but my room has what I affectionately call a nook that I've set up as my workspace.

Tears of frustration well up as the stubborn lug nut refuses to budge even a smidge. I blow my hair out of my eyes as I grunt, "Come on, you stupid fucker!"

"Has that ever worked for you? Swearing at something that can't fight back, I mean?" The deep, raspy voice coming from above where I'm squatting has me literally falling back on my ass, as I squeal in surprise.

"Sweet porcupine quills," I shrilly squeak out, looking up at the man who has appeared from out of nowhere. "Warn a girl next time before you scare the hell out of her, why dontcha?!"

"Sweetheart, I called out to you several times as I approached," he says in defense. "Surprised you didn't hear the roaring of my bike."

Glancing behind him, I see a massive motorcycle parked behind my Jeep. It's got a custom paint job from what I can tell, and the chrome is so shiny and reflective that I could apply my makeup perfectly if I was so inclined. "Huh. Yeah, guess I was laser focused on what I was doing," I reply, pointing at the offending lug nut.

I can't see his eyes or even his face as he's wearing one of those gaiter face masks that covers him up from his jaw to his neck with an opening in between, and he's sporting a pair of wraparound aviator sunglasses, so his eye color isn't visible either. His helmet is sitting on the leather seat of his bike, and I watch with great interest as he pulls his gloves off his hands and slides them into his pocket.

"How about I give you a hand then so you can get back on the road?" he asks once his hands are freed from their confinement. "Looks like you got all but one taken off, huh?"

"Yeah, for some reason, this one is being stubborn," I stammer out. Right now, my tongue is so dang tied as I watch him crouch down and hold out his hand. Holy shit! It's a real live biker! Realizing he wants the tool I'm holding, I manage to hand it to him without dropping it even though my entire body is trembling in excitement, barely managing to hold back the shocked gasp when I feel my skin tingle from our touch.

I'm unsure what he does differently than I did, other than having brute strength where I don't, but within a few seconds, the lug nut I could've sworn was gorilla glued onto the stud is laying on the ground and he's removing my flat. Standing up, I notice how powerfully built he is; his thighs are thick, probably bigger than both of mine together. When I see his muscles bulge while lifting my spare, I nearly moan out loud.

Keep it together, Tressa. Jeez, you'd think you've never seen a good-looking guy before, you dummy!

"I like that Jeep gives you a regular sized tire and not one of those fucking donuts," he says while replacing each lug nut one by one and tightening it down before he moves on to the next.

"Yeah, that's one of the reasons why I got it," I admit. I'm searching my brain for something, anything else to say so he'll keep talking when he hands me the tool then stands back up.

"Want me to put that one in the back for you? Looks like you picked up a nail, but you've got a shit ton of tread left so you should get it patched instead of tossing it."

"Um, yeah, that would be great. Thanks." Wow... what a conversationalist I am.

Since his back is to me, he can't see me roll my eyes at my lame response. By the time he turns back around, I'm standing there, wringing my hands. I still can't make out his face, but I think he's undoubtedly grinning at me because it looks like his eyes are crinkling from the side of his sunglasses.

"You're all set. Be careful," he states.

"Can I pay you for helping me?" I ask.

"Absofuckinlutely not," he growls out. The tone sends a delicious shiver through me as I imagine him using it while saying something else far more carnal to me.

Wishful thinking. There's no way on this earth someone who looks like he does would ever notice the likes of me.

"I didn't mean to offend you," I rush to say in my defense. "I just know I'd still be sitting here, cursing at my tire, if you hadn't stopped to help. I'd probably have called roadside assistance if you hadn't stopped."

I see him shake his head a little before he replies, "No offense taken. Go ahead and get in your car, I'll wait to pull out until I see you're safely back on the road."

"Thank you."

"You're welcome, darling. Now, there's a break in traffic so you best get to hauling your ass into your car."

"I'm TELLING YOU, NICOLE, IT WAS LIKE A SCENE OUT of one of our books," I exclaim, having called her as soon as I was back on the road. "Mr. Tall, Dark, and Handsome stops to help a lowly, stranded female."

Her giggle rings through my car and I join in. "Yeah, I know I'm being silly. Heck, I didn't even see his face because he was wearing one of those face cover thingies we see mentioned in MC novels."

"Can you be more specific?" she teases. "Thingies covers a wide range of things, Tress."

"You know, the kind of mask that covers their throat and the bottom part of their face?"

"Ah, a gaiter mask. Bet he looked hot." I knew what I meant but couldn't remember the word, however, I'm still soaring, riding the high from my encounter with the kind of man I've dreamed about since discovering the MC genre.

"Add in the wraparound sunglasses, the well-worn jeans, the leather jacket, and yeah, I'd say so," I admit.

"I wish I had been able to go with you," she whines.

"Next time, promise me you will. It feels weird not having you with me," I say, pleading for her to make vows even though at this point, it's a fictionalized venue.

"As soon as we know when the next one is going to be, I'll put my time in for those days off, okay?" she asks. "Now, I gotta run. You stay safe, my friend, and feel free to spam me with an influx of pictures with all the hotties you meet!"

"I will."

Once the call disconnects, my podcast comes back on, and I'm soon lost in another episode of *Crime Junkies* which dissects the details of cold cases where the person is either missing or was found dead. Nicole thinks I'm weird because I can listen to these, binge watch *Forensic Files* and most of the shows on the ID channel, but I cannot handle horror flicks.

Nope, not this chicken. I don't like watching blood and gore, and I've tried explaining that these shows usually don't show graphic pictures, but she doesn't believe me. As the miles pass by, my mind flits to and fro about the upcoming weekend.

I just hope I'm brave enough to actually *speak* to people. Learning at an early age to be seen and not heard, I've had the hardest time breaking free from my protective bubble because I'm afraid people will treat me the way my step-monster did, with derision and scorn. Sometimes I wonder why she married my dad since he never made it a secret that he had a child, then, I realize for her, it was more about the bank account he had acquired than any enduring love story.

My dad tried, and when he wasn't gone on a business trip, we spent a lot of time together where he taught me how to fish, how to do basic maintenance on my car, and how to ballroom dance. It was something he enjoyed doing with my mom when she was alive, so he taught me.

Still, his attention definitely didn't overshadow Nancy's vindictive treatment of me, that's for sure. I'm unsure if the reason she hated me so much was because I looked so much like my mom or not, but I suspect that may be the case since my dad never made any bones about the fact she was the love of his life.

I start to slow when my GPS indicates my turn is up ahead, excitement now thrumming through me.

"It's almost time," I quietly shriek in my car. Does that make me dorky? Probably so, but I don't care at all. As I continue to follow the directions, I make note of the various places to eat since my plan is to check in, get a shower, then find some food before tonight's meet and greet at the venue.

Once I find my hotel and park, I carry everything in except my cart since I'll need it tomorrow to haul around my books. Checking in, I spot M Merin and Kristine Allen, two of the authors I've made covers for in the past.

"Keep it cool, Tressa," I mumble to myself as I wait in line behind them while they check in. Kristine appears to have a large entourage, which is kind of neat. I know from being in her reader group that her husband is a bona fide member of a club. From what I've seen on her online post, he, and some of his brothers sometimes come with her to signings.

Aside from the guy who stopped to help me this morning, I've never been around any real-life bikers, so I hope I can keep from acting too goofy around them. I'll be checking the corners of my mouth periodically to make sure I'm not drooling. Nicole says that my goofiness is part of my charm, that someone out there won't care that I'm slightly awkward, often quiet, and definitely shy, but I haven't met him yet, so I think she's just trying to placate me. Until he materializes, I'll keep to my book boyfriends and live vicariously through the heroines.

CHAPTER TWO

Chaos

Thoughts of the woman I helped on the side of the highway run through my head as I make my way to our clubhouse. I saw the way her eyes widened when we lightly touched, but more importantly, I *felt* the zing of familiarity which makes no sense to me. Not only that, but the scent of lilacs and grass after it's been freshly mowed was present, which makes no sense to me at all. No clue why, but Fox called church and stated it was imperative we all show up. Most of the time, if we're working or out on a run we can get a pass, but not this time.

Pulling into the clubhouse, I carefully walk my bike back into my designated spot, then put my helmet in my saddlebag before I lock it up. Not that anyone would dare fuck with anything that's within the boundaries of our property, but old habits are tough to overcome and hard to break. I pull my gaiter down and take in a deep breath of fresh, clean air, before making my way inside.

As I stop at the bar, I see Teeny pull out a bottle of beer for me. "Thanks, babe," I say, before popping the top and taking a long drink. Before I've got it finished, she has a second one pulled and ready for me. I grab the fresh bottle once I've emptied the one I was working on, then head to the room we use for church.

The Zephyr Hills Phantoms MC started about forty years ago, when a group of wolf shifters decided they wanted to live life on their terms, and have the camaraderie of others like themselves. All of us come from packs throughout the United States, although for each of us, the reason why we've joined is our own. Growing up as the alpha's son, I knew it would be a long time before I would potentially take over and lead my family's pack, partially due to our longevity, but also because I am the second-born son, and unless the first-born male declines the leadership role and leaves the pack, it won't pass down to me unless something nefarious takes his life. Unfortunately, because I have alpha tendencies and my brother is an asshole who's threatened by my natural instincts to protect those weaker than me, and to keep the pack unified while living a peaceful existence, I knew it was time to leave because being forced to stay under his reign was something I couldn't handle. He's spiteful and would gain happiness over my misery.

So, I bought a motorcycle, broke ties with my pack, and hit the open road, finally landing in Zephyr Hills, Texas. Pretty mountain scenery, plenty of trees, and the opportunity to be on the ground floor of a new motorcycle club has kept me here with no desire to leave.

I still talk to my family from time to time, of course, but pack politics was never my thing so this lifestyle, while foreign to my parents, suits me just fine. Making my way into the room, I see there are a few others we're still waiting on to show, so I plop down into my chair, nudge Fox in the shoulder, then promptly light up a cigarette, motioning to Ogre to slide one of the ashtrays in my direction.

"Thought you'd have been here by now," Fox says. He doesn't attempt to be quiet; there's no reason for it since we're all shifters and can hear the slightest murmur. That trait has come in handy a few times because we're a well-kept secret among humans. Thankfully, the room we use for church is soundproof, as are our rooms. It's bad enough I see enough of my brothers' naked asses in the common room, I don't need to hear them getting off too.

They don't know we exist, and we don't share that information except on an as-needed basis.

"Would've been here earlier, but I stopped to help a stranded woman change her tire," I reply, blowing out a perfect ring of smoke.

"When you gonna teach me how to do that?" Sly, our VP, asks me.

"When your balls drop," I retort, snickering.

"I got your balls dropping," he sneers, grabbing his junk and thrusting his hips toward me.

"Please, fucker, stop trying to overcompensate," I say just as Stealth enters the room, looks around, then closes the door.

Before Sly can say another word, Fox slams the gavel against the table and all talking ceases.

He sighs, then says, "Fuck, I love the absolute silence doing that causes." He smirks when we all burst into laughter then grows solemn once again.

"Okay, so there's an indie author, Sapphire Knight, who is hosting a huge event in Lake Conroe this weekend, called Motorcycles, Mobsters, and Mayhem. She reached out to the dominant club in our area and got our name and contact information, along with several other clubs, as folks who might want to attend."

"What the fuck? *Why?*" Sly asks, looking around the table.

"She wants to have real members of clubs attend so the readers can get the full experience or some shit," Fox replies, pulling his own smoke out of a pack and lighting it up. "Guess the guys they use on their covers are mostly non-bikers, although I recognize a few."

"How did *you* see them?" Ogre questions, smirking at Fox.

"Went on the website for the event, fucker. They've got a list of the authors attending and some of them apparently write motorcycle club romance, so I clicked links to scan and see what popped up," Fox mutters, glaring around the table when we all burst out in roars of laughter.

"Are all the clubs planning to attend friendlies of ours?" I question, not wanting to have a turf war break out among a bunch of unsuspecting and innocent civilians.

"Yeah, brother, they are. The dominant even reached out to the fucking Bastians to advise them to steer clear and have offered their own club up as security for the event. Think Ms. Knight took them up on it when she was informed there was a club in the area that was bad news."

"Well, at least she knows who *not* to invite," Ogre states, now snickering. He's not wrong, though, the Bastians are the very definition of evil, through and through. "What do you need from us?"

"A few volunteers," Fox replies. "If I don't get any, then I'll make it a mandatory order and you won't have a choice."

Grinning, I raise my hand. "Why not? Who knows, maybe our mates will be there," I jeer. There's always a silver lining to be found on something you don't want to do if you dig for it.

Unlikely, but possible. Who knows? We typically don't find our mates among humans, but it has happened, but since I spend most of my time around these fuckers, I don't get out and around many of the female persuasion, human or shifter.

The club sweet butts definitely don't count as far as I'm concerned. In fact, I prefer to go without pussy rather than stick my dick where my brothers have gone before. I'll let them suck me off from time to time, but actual sex? Yeah, no. Not my cup of tea at all. So what if I have a monthly subscription for lube?

"Fine, Chaos, Ogre, Sly, you three have volunteered for this chore," Fox decrees. "The rest of you fuckers, make sure you stay sober in case anything happens and we're needed."

"Pres, you know we don't get drunk," Ledger says.

"I know that fucker, but once y'all start partying, you tend to get lost in pussy, and if one of our brothers finds trouble or it finds them, we need to be ready to roll the fuck out," Fox growls, his wolf staring down the table at Ledger.

"Alright, alright," Ledger retorts, waving his hands in the air. "No excessive alcohol until the boys are back under our roof."

"That's correct."

Wanting to grab a shower to wash off the road grime, I ask, "What else, Pres?"

"That was it. I'll text y'all with the location and times. Best behavior, brothers."

"So, no wolfing out, got it," Ogre teases. "Just when I was gonna show off my handsome physique too."

"Asshole, you know better," Fox bellows. "This signing is likely to be attended by *humans* and I highly doubt there'll be any shifters or mates roaming around. Make nice, take pictures, hell, take them for a fucking ride on your bike, *not your cock*, if you have to. I don't want any issues with the dominant, you hear me?"

I shake my head at Ogre's antics. He's a huge motherfucker, but overall, relatively docile, unless he gets riled up. Then he resembles his namesake from that kid's movie, practically hulking out as he destroys whatever is in his path.

Granted, my road name is indicative of my personality as well. I prefer to observe what's going on around me and don't rush to snap judgments, but when shit hits the fan, I tend to lose my shit and go berserk, creating and causing chaos in my midst.

Fox slams the gavel down and yells, "Church dismissed. Let's go have a cold one, brothers."

———

"FINALLY, SOME PEACE AND QUIET," I MUTTER AS I enter my room. We're a small club with only twelve members, although two are prospects right now.

That's how we want it, however, since we try to stay on the right side of the law. We don't make waves, but we also don't take any shit from anyone either. Deciding I want to go for a run and let my wolf play, I head back downstairs and out the back door. Our property is surrounded by woods on one side, a mountain on the other, and a river at the back. Plenty of space to run amuck as well as hunt for prey. Quickly stripping down, I set my clothes on one of the chairs on the deck then quickly shift.

Where once a man stood, now my caramel-coated wolf stands. We're larger than a regular wolf born in the wild, but I know if a human sees us, they won't know the difference.

Sniffing the air, I scent a deer near the river so start loping in that direction.

I'm not particularly hungry, so I won't kill it. I just want to keep my tracking skills up because that's my job as the club enforcer.

It's my duty to protect my brothers and everyone under our roof. So, I frequently practice tracking various animals in order to keep my skills sharp.

Once I arrive at the river, I decide to shift back to my human form and swim. I'll still shower after I return to my room, but the night air, coupled with the cool breeze, soothes me for some reason. I'm not sure what has me so out of sorts; I was fine earlier today during my ride. But ever since I came across that woman and helped her, I've felt off kilter.

Shaking my head, I swim until the air cools even more then shift again to my wolf, and return to the clubhouse. Time to get myself ready for bed because this weekend's going to be a long one from the sound of it.

CHAPTER THREE

TRESSA

"TRESSA? IS THAT YOU?" KRISTINE ASKS, TURNING toward me.

"Hey, how are you?" I reply, smiling at her. She was the first author to give me a chance at creating her covers, and ever since, unless she's writing in a world that requires her to use a specific cover designer, I've made them for her.

She engulfs me in a hug, laughing. "We finally get to meet! Marty, come here, this is my fucking phenomenal cover designer."

I find myself in another set of arms and look up to see her husband smiling down at me. "Hey."

"Hey yourself, darling. You do my girl proud," he replies, finally releasing me. "Both of them because I claim Merin as well."

"Don't think my hubby would like that much," Merin retorts, grinning at me. "Hey, Tressa. We were definitely looking forward to meeting you this weekend. Have you gotten checked in yet?"

"No, not yet," I manage to stammer. I feel so out of my element right now, I'm kind of wishing that the ground would open up and swallow me whole.

No such luck, however, as I'm called to the front desk.

"We were just going to eat here in the restaurant, do you want to join us?" Kristine asks.

"I'd love to. Um, how long? I had to change my tire on the way so wanted to grab a shower," I admit.

"How about an hour, does that give you enough time?" she questions.

"Sounds good to me. See you then."

After checking in, I make my way to my room, stunned at how nice the hotel actually is, but not surprised since Nicole's employed by one of the bigger hotel chains. Once inside, I quickly pull out clean clothes and my hygiene bag then get in the shower. Since my hair is still good, I pile it on top of my head with a clip as I step under the steaming water, my mind still on the man I met earlier.

"Get him out of your head, girl," I say as I quickly lather my body then rinse. "He'd never be interested in the likes of you."

Once out of the shower, I moisturize my face, lotion my body, then put on clean clothes before taking the time to style my hair and apply some makeup. I may not wear it often, but since I'll be eating with authors I admire and work for, I decide it's worth taking the time to do.

"Okay, I've still got about twenty minutes before I have to get downstairs, so let's get unpacked and make sure we have our stuff all together and in one place for tomorrow."

Within minutes, I have my cpap machine set up, drinks from the cooler stored in the mini fridge, snacks on the small desk that's tucked in the corner, and my list of preorders to pick up in the morning nestled inside of my purse for safe keeping. Slipping cash and my ID into my pocket, I grab my phone and room key before I head downstairs.

Time to get out of my shell a bit.

"I LOVE THE COVERS YOU'VE DESIGNED FOR ME," Kristine enthuses as we sip on our drinks while waiting for our meals to come out.

"I enjoy doing them," I confess, grabbing a chip and dipping it into my personal bowl of salsa.

"Well, good, because unless I have to use a particular designer for a world I'm writing in, I don't want to lose you," she professes.

"Did you place a lot of preorders?" Merin questions. The two of us are drinking the biggest margaritas I've ever seen, and I worry about getting buzzed.

Giggling, I nod. "Yeah, I did. My roommate and I put two bookshelves together before I left to head here," I admit. "I just hope I didn't go overboard."

"Eh, we all do," Kristine states, her words come out with an air of nonchalance. "Even us authors run around grabbing signed pretties from our friends. Especially those of us writing in the RBMC world where we have characters crossing over."

"I freaking love that whole concept," I confess.

Apparently, get a little tequila in me and I become a chatterbox. They're going to think I'm a dork.

"It's definitely been a lot of fun to write," Merin adds. "Everyone's chapter is just a little bit different, and of course, some have paranormal aspects, like Kristine's guys."

I slowly nod. "I saw where one of the authors used several different characters from a variety of different clubs when their city's chapter was patched over. It was a cool read and I fell in love with y'all's guys even more."

"So, any guy in your life we need to watch out for?" Kristine's husband, Marty, asks, shocking the hell out of me.

"Um, no. Single here, just a roommate and her crazy fur babies," I reply.

"No fucking way," he says, acting shocked. "Well, we'll keep an eye out because from what we understand, there are a lot of clubs who are going to be in attendance. Don't need some asshole finding his balls and taking his shot, especially if we think he's not good enough."

I nearly spit my drink out at his words. "Me? Uh, just to say, I'm the proverbial wallflower. My roommate was the one who encouraged me to come to this, especially since so many of the authors I create covers or edit for are here."

"Well, whoever told you that was a fucking liar," he states, narrowing his eyes in thought. Looking at his wife, he asks, "Am I right?"

"Yes, dear," she teases, smirking at her man. Turning to me, she grows serious. "Tressa, you've got that All-American, girl next door look, and trust me, these men like that kind of thing."

Oh, jellybeans. I wasn't expecting anything of the sort to be an issue.

"Uh, I'm not sure I'm prepared for any kind of attention," I admit. Changing the subject, I ask Kristine, "Did you get a chance to look over the mock-up I sent you the other day?"

"No, not yet. I had to work my day job then make sure I had all my pre orders packed and ready to go so Marty could get us loaded up."

"Well, when you do, let me know what you think. And as always, if I need to change something, let me know."

Merin pops up and conveys, "Sapphire just posted in the author group that we can set up tonight if we'd like."

"Hell yeah! Then we don't have to get up as early. Do you want to go and help us, Tressa?"

"Sure, why not?"

I've always been curious about the stuff that goes on behind the scenes of a book event and it looks like I'll get a chance to assuage my curiosity. I can't wait to call Nicole later and fill her in on the details.

"GO AHEAD, TAKE YOUR PRE ORDER NOW," LIBERTY insists. "That way, you can spend your time tomorrow actually talking to authors, buying other books, and hooking yourself more cover as well as editing clients."

"Are you sure?" I question, having already received my pre orders from Kristine, Merin, Nikki Landis, DM Earl, and Sapphire Knight. The only reason I stopped by Liberty's table is because she didn't have her latest release on the preorder form, and I wanted to see if she would have any available for me to purchase on Saturday.

"Positive. Tomorrow is going to be an absolute insane asylum. One year, Darlene came with me as a reader, and she literally spent her whole time picking up pre orders for herself and several other friends who couldn't make it. She didn't get to talk to anyone for any length of time or catch up with our online friends and these signings are meant to allow you to chit chat with folks."

"Oh! I wonder if I can get mine from her too! She's the last one on my preorder list. I've got a list of other books I want but I didn't want to go too crazy with my pre orders."

"I'm sure she'll let you. She's just over there."

"Thanks, Liberty. Maybe tomorrow we can get a picture together?"

She laughs while looking down at her outfit, which consists of shorts, a tank top, and flip-flops. "Yeah, I'll be show ready tomorrow so don't forget because we don't always remember."

"I will, and thanks again!"

I walk over to where Darlene Tallman is setting up and hear her talking to the woman I presume is her assistant. "Since we have two tables, I think my solo books and series should be on one table, and all of my co-writes should go on the other one, what do you think, Renee?"

"I think that'll work," her assistant replies. "Dar, you've got someone here."

She turns to me and smiles. "Hey, how are you? Are you a reader, an assistant, or an author? I don't recognize you, but that's not unusual considering the sheer number of people running around right now."

"I'm a reader who also designs covers for several of the authors here. I also edit and beta read."

"Really? Do you have a card? I love my cover designer so likely won't change, but I'm a sucker for premades and I'm always on the lookout for folks to join my team. Some are more like proofers, others I consider readers, and then the rest actually notice plot holes and stuff."

"I do! I almost didn't bring them, but my roommate convinced me to in case someone asked."

"I'm glad you did. Trust me, by the end of the signing, I'll have a stack of business cards from folks who are going to stop by my table."

"Really? For what kind of things?" My curiosity is now roused, and I wait eagerly to hear what she's got to say.

"Swag, audiobooks, editing, formatting, cover design, you name it. If it involves any aspect of a book, someone will be here peddling what they do," she says. "Of course, I've managed to find some awesome swag makers that way, so it's definitely beneficial. Plus, a lot of times, they buy a book or two so it's a win-win, right?"

While she continues to talk, she's sorting through a bunch of tote bags with her logo on them, and I briefly wonder if those are her preorders.

"Did she have a preorder, Dar?" Renee asks.

"That's what I'm looking for," she replies, laughing. "I swear to God, all of this was organized until we started setting up. Ah, here it is!" she says triumphantly, holding up my bag.

"Now, I personalized them because that's what you asked for, right?"

"Yes. I did, and thank you. My roomie and I built two book-shelves for the books I'm bringing home."

"I think I'm up to five at home myself."

"Really?"

"Girl, I'll always be a reader first even though I now write and publish my own stories! Like everyone else who you'll see here, my love for words is strong. Can I ask you which book of mine you like best or is that putting you on the spot?"

I stop to think about what she's asking me. Each of her standalone books has called to something inside, whether it was how the heroine overcame some physical obstacle or health issue, or how they rose up after being crushed. "I love them all but really enjoyed *Her Kinsman Redeemer.*"

"Really? I actually got the idea for it while in church one Sunday," she says, giggling. "There I was, half an ear on the pastor's sermon, back in the book of Ruth rereading her story and using the characteristics she and Boaz had to create a contemporary romance. I almost felt bad except for the fact that if I wasn't supposed to write it, I wouldn't have had the idea then, right?"

"Are you ever going to write about any of the other couples?" I question.

"I'm not sure. Originally, I had planned to, but with two different friends I cowrite with, plus my own solo series I'm working on, I don't know where I'd fit the time in to conquer their stories."

Renee starts laughing and states, "You don't really need sleep, do you?"

"Good grief, yes I do, I get these awful dark circles and the cats hate when I'm up and down because I disrupt their sleep."

"Tell them more books equals more snacks and wet food," Renee advises.

"Whatever. Tressa, I hope you have a fantastic time this weekend. Thanks for stopping by and chatting with us for a few minutes. Be sure to stop tomorrow so we can get a picture because for sure, I'm a hot mess right now."

"I will, thank you again."

I make my way back over to Kristine's table since I rode over with them, my arms laden down with my preorder bags. Tomorrow, I'll have my cart, but that'll be for new purchases.

"I see you managed to grab all your preorders, huh?" Kristine asks as she rummages through a box.

"Yeah, everyone was so nice about it," I reply. "Anything I can do to help? Merin has Alia helping her and doesn't need me."

"We just have to finish stacking the books," she says, "then we'll be ready to head back to the hotel."

"Well, let me give you a hand because I'm sure you've got things to do there."

She starts laughing. "Yeah, need to finish putting my preorder bags together."

IT DIDN'T TAKE US LONG TO FINISH SETTING HER table up, and now, I'm back in my hotel room, Nicole on the phone as we discuss my plan of attack for Saturday since I've got all my preorders picked up.

"Are you having a good time? You sound like you are, at least," she says.

I stop and think about it, and realize since I arrived, I've talked and laughed more than I can remember.

"You know something? I *am* having a good time and can't wait to meet other authors tomorrow."

"Don't forget to hand out your business cards," she reminds me. "Who knows? You could end up building an empire or something, especially since the ones you already work for are enthusiastically thrilled with your work."

"I won't, I promise. So, are there any books you want me to get for you?"

She rattles off several books she wants, which I dutifully jot down, before saying she needed to go. After telling her good night and plugging my phone into the charger, I get up and go through my suitcase so I can figure out what outfit I want to wear the next day.

CHAPTER FOUR

CHAOS

"Sorry, babe, just not feeling it tonight," I tell Renda, gently pushing her off my dick. "Go find another brother."

"You sure, Chaos? You look a little tense," she replies, standing up while swiping her hand across her mouth as I tuck my dick back into my pants.

"I'll be fine, get now, babe," I demand, hardening my tone.

Sometimes our sweet butts tend to push the issue, but as the club's Enforcer, I refuse to allow *anyone* to try that shit with me. As she walks away, muttering under her breath, I realize she's threatening my life. My wolf takes notice and wants to shred her into a million pieces, but I soothe him, promising another long run so he can work out his aggression.

"You gonna run?" Ogre asks, walking up to me, a beer bottle pinched between his fingers.

"Yeah, not feeling this shit tonight," I confess. "Better to get out and run it out than start some shit I'll end up having to finish, y'know?"

He barks out a laugh while nodding. "Fuck yeah, I get it. I think sometimes it's because so many of the brothers have alpha blood in them, don't you?"

"Never really thought about it, Ogre. You wanna run?"

We usually run together as a whole pack, but on Friday nights when the booze is flowing, the music is loud, and the pussy is practically everywhere, it's not as common. Of course, since we're wolves, we don't necessarily have to go anywhere as a group.

"Yeah, sure. I'll go see if anyone else wants to join in, but if not, I'll have your back, Brother."

I head out toward the back deck and strip down, quickly shifting into my wolf while I wait for Ogre and whoever else he corrals to join me. It's not long before Fox, Ogre, Sly, and

Ledger come out, quickly shedding their clothes before they shift.

Looks like we're going to go for a run.

———

HOURS LATER, WHICH INCLUDED ANOTHER SWIM IN the creek, we're back on the deck, grabbing our clothes, and heading inside. Thankfully, nudity isn't an issue with shifters because I have no fucking desire to put my clothes on when I'm literally going to take a hot as hell shower then pass out for a few hours before I get ready to go to the shindig.

Once in my room, since my clothes weren't really dirty, I set them to the side then head into my shower. Despite two long runs, I still feel somewhat unsettled and that has my senses wide open and on high alert. Now would be the perfect time, with our attention distracted by this event we're attending, for the Bastians to do something.

"Kinda wish the dominant hadn't reached out to them," I mutter to myself as the hot water sluices over my body. "Now they know there are vulnerable people in town, and with the barbaric shit they're into, we're going to have to be on our fucking toes without letting the humans know we exist."

As I shave, and then finish my normal nightly routine, I hear a knock on my door. Tightening the towel slung low on my hips, I go to it and open it to see Teeny standing there.

"What do you want?" I question, my tone coming across as hard and unyielding.

"I um, well, I know you went for two runs today so thought I'd come and see if you needed to relieve a little tension," she coyly states.

Only my innate control has me managing not to roll my eyes. "Teeny, when have I ever turned to you or any of the other club girls to ease my stress?" I ask. "That's right, hardly ever, and I sure as fuck never invite any of you into my room."

Now, if I want to be sucked off, the common room is fine. While I'm not keen on fucking one of them, I have no compunction about using their mouths when the urge over-comes me. As far as her coming to my room, I'm kind of stymied to be honest. This is my den, my sanctuary. My wolf and I are in agreement that other than letting them in to clean, no woman, except our mate, will ever share this space with us.

She hangs her head, an embarrassed flush covering her face and upper chest, which is showing thanks to her barely-there halter top she's wearing. "I'm sorry, Chaos," she whispers, now uncomfortable since my wolf is peering at her and he's definitely an alpha who takes no shit.

"If I wanted one of you to suck my dick, I would've stayed downstairs," I coldly inform her. "Now, get. I'm sure one of the others will take you up on your generous offer."

As I shut my door, I hear her practically running down the stairs and back toward the common room, making me chuckle.

"That was harsh, Brother," Fox says from outside my door.

Opening it back again, I see him standing there, freshly showered himself. Shrugging, I let him in knowing he probably wants to talk about Saturday's event.

"What can I say, Fox? All those bitches should know better by now," I retort, tossing my towel onto my bed as I grab a pair of sweats and slip them on.

"Wanted to talk about tomorrow," he states.

"Figured as much. Anything I need to be prepared for?" I question, leaning against the wall.

"Okay, so I fell down a rabbit hole where book signings are concerned, and actually found some videos online of different ones. Some of the attendees can get a little touchy-feely, so you and the boys make sure you keep your wolves in check," he warns.

"How close are we talking?" I ask, mentally cringing at the thought of strangers doing that to me. Being groped by complete strangers will have me battling my wolf in order to keep him contained.

"Dirty dancing close," he replies, snickering.

"You sure you don't wanna come with us seeing as you're the *president?*" I goad.

"That's the nice thing about my position, I can delegate," he retorts. "Seriously, I'm a bit worried that the Bastians might try to pull a fast one, so I'm debating sending one of the prospects with our van in the event they do so y'all can get them away from the readers without anyone being the wiser."

I grin, but there's no humor behind it. "Let those fuckers try to hurt anyone in our neck of the woods. They may be strangers, but from the sound of it, most of them are female and it's innately in our DNA to protect them from undue harm."

"True, true. I also noticed you're not yourself. Anything you care to share, Brother?"

I slowly shake my head, unwilling to explain my uneasiness to him. It's bad enough he's intuitive enough that he sensed something is off with me. "I'm good, Fox."

"If that changes..."

"You'll be the first to know," I promise.

"Alright then. Good talk," he jests, walking out of my room. I smirk at his tone, because he tries to come across as a hardass, but in reality, he has his finger on all of our pulses, which is one of the reasons he's such a good leader for the lot of us.

Time to get some shut eye; no clue what Saturday's gonna hold, but I need to be well-rested and prepared.

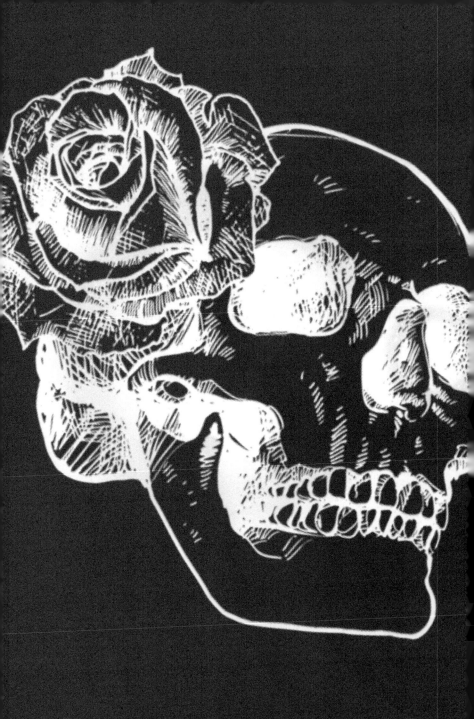

CHAPTER FIVE

TRESSA

"OH, MY GOD, IT'S FINALLY TIME!" I MURMUR WHEN my alarm goes off bright and early Saturday morning.

The meet and greet was a lot of fun, and surprisingly, I took more pictures than I expected. Not only that, but it was like I found my people, because I was a veritable chatterbox most of the night. And since I only had two drinks, I know it wasn't alcohol courage speaking.

Throwing the covers back, I remove my cpap mask, and after quickly straightening my bed, I hurry into the bathroom to begin getting ready. One fast shower later, and I'm putting on the event T-shirt I ordered from B&D Sassy

Kreations, a company two friends started to design items for authors. The shirt is adorable; it's got a girl sitting on a stack of books and several of them have author names they create items for on the spines. I debate again about wearing jeans versus capris, then decide to wear the capris since I've heard it can get hot in the event room. Dancing around my room in excitement, I grab a cold drink from my mini fridge, then sit down at the vanity to do my hair and apply some makeup.

Not much, because I feel far more comfortable wearing a more natural look, but I know I'm going to want selfies with people today, and I want to take one step forward and look my best. As I dry my hair, using the new products my hair-dresser suggested that's supposed to help tame the wayward curls that get worse with humidity, I idly listen to the local news. I don't know why because it's not as if I have a vested interest in this area, but some of the stories make me laugh, especially the one where a local high school's seniors played a prank that made all the fountains spray the school colors.

Finally satisfied with how I look, I pack it all away so it's neat and organized once again, then begin gathering what I'll need for the rest of the day. I bought a small, insulated lunchbox and quickly pack it with several drinks, then I double check my purse to ensure I have my ticket printed out, as well as my extra money. Slipping on my comfortable sneakers, I gather everything in my arms, including the 'Do Not Disturb' sign, and leave my room, hanging it on the outside knob.

Nini and I saw some show where a detective recommended doing that if you were traveling alone, so I promised her I would follow his advice. I make my way to the vending area, put some ice in the gallon-size Ziploc bag I brought, and then I head out to where I parked Ruby the night before.

I KNOW I'M RIDICULOUSLY EARLY, SO I SWING through a McDonald's and order an egg McMuffin and a bottle of orange juice. As my music blares, I quickly eat so I can sing along. I think this is the most fun I've ever had all by myself and wish Nicole had been able to come with me.

"Maybe next time," I murmur just as my phone rings. Seeing it's her, I answer only to hear her giggling.

"You just ate your breakfast, didn't you?" she teases, still laughing.

"I think we know each other too well," I retort before I burst into giggles. "Yeah, I did."

"Are you wearing capris or jeans?"

"I decided on the capris because I remembered reading in the attendee group that sometimes the room gets hot."

"Don't forget to take lots of pictures!"

"I won't, I promise. I really wish you were here, though. I'm having fun, but it's not the same."

"Next time," she swears. "Because I wish I was there too. Did you see they're going to have real live bikers there? Some of the local clubs or something like that."

I briefly wonder if the guy who helped me out will be there then push that thought away. He was probably just riding through. Although to be honest, it's not like I'd know if he was there since his face was covered and I don't remember what the back of his leather jacket said.

But you do *remember how tall he was, what color his hair and beard were, and the fact he had gauges in his ears,* my memory whispers.

"Oh, how exciting! I'll probably turn into an even bigger dork than I usually am if any of them are really good looking," I jest.

"You're not a dork, Tressa! Just because you're shy doesn't make you one," she admonishes.

"How many dates have I been on since you've known me?" I ask. "That's right. One."

"He was a jerk."

She's right, but even still, his cruel words still occasionally play on repeat in my head. Awkward. Lesbo. Prude. Shaking my head of those bad memories, I return to our conversation.

"I've got it all planned out, I think," I tell her. "I picked up all of our preorders last night and they're safely stored inside Ruby. So I'll go to each table, grab some swag, probably buy more books, get pictures, and try to forget that my best friend is at home."

"You're going to have a ton of fun, Tress," she insists. "Oh, by the way, check your PayPal account. You did bring your card, didn't you?"

"I did and what did you do?"

"Happy early birthday!" she exclaims, giggling.

"Nini, my birthday was last month, you goof."

"I didn't say *which* birthday, now did I?" she teases.

"Whatever," I grumble, causing her to laugh harder as I pull into the venue and park. "Okay, I'm here so I want to get inside and get a place in line."

"Have fun! I miss you!"

"Miss you too. I'll call when I'm back in the room tonight."

"You better!"

I'M ONE OF THE FIRST PEOPLE TO LINE UP, SO I MAKE myself comfortable, plug my phone into the power charger I brought with me so I'm ready to go, then start people watching, as it appears some of the authors are just coming in to get their tables set up. I can't wait to see how the room is transformed; last night, about half of the authors were inside setting up, but once the rest of them are done, I'm sure it's going to resemble a book lover's dream.

"Hey, can you watch my stuff while I run to the restroom?"

I look to my left where the voice came from and see a woman with her own cart standing there, waiting for me to answer. "Sure, not a problem," I reply.

I had wanted to get a wagon, but spacing wouldn't permit it, so instead, I bought what Nicole and I call a granny cart. It's upright but will fold flat once I'm done with it and we managed to find an insert so that any books I get won't get damaged by the wire. I love it because I have my insulated bag over the back of the handle for easy access in case I get thirsty.

"Great! My name's Tracy."

"Tressa. Go ahead and go, I've got you covered," I promise. She grins before practically running across the way to where the restrooms are located. Hopefully, she won't mind watching my stuff when I do the same since all the liquid I've been drinking seems to be congregating in my bladder.

I continue my people watching until Tracy returns then grin at her. "My turn," I state, standing and stretching.

"Hurry, because I think I heard they're going to start letting us in soon," she replies, which causes me to move a lot quicker than I intended.

"Oof," I say, after crashing into a muscular body and nearly falling on my ass.

"You in a hurry, darlin'?" the smooth, raspy voice asks as he grabs onto my arms to keep me upright.

"Um, yeah, kind of. They're going to start letting the VIPs in soon and I wanted to make sure I was back before then," I admit, blushing because I'm standing in front of the ladies restroom.

"Well, I won't keep you. I hope you enjoy today," he replies, winking at me.

I hurry inside and take care of business, the whole time mentally berating myself at how stupid I probably sounded.

DARLENE TALLMAN

Rushing back to where Tracy is now standing by our stuff, I thank her, and take the handle of my cart.

"I hope we have a great time today," she whispers, practically vibrating with her excitement.

"Me too," I reply.

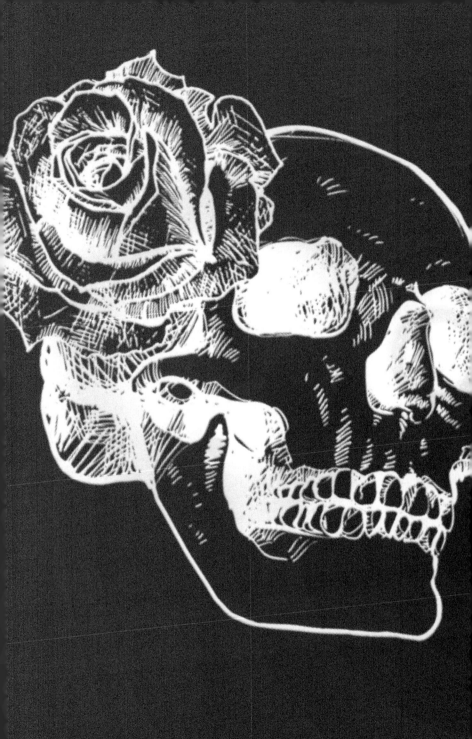

CHAPTER SIX

CHAOS

NEVER IN MY WILDEST DREAMS WOULD I HAVE imagined practically catching my mate before she landed on her ass. Yet, as she scurries into the ladies room, her face flushed a deep pink, I stand here feeling poleaxed.

Many years ago, when I was much younger and still lived with my family of origin, I remember my great-grandmother talking about what happens when you find your mate. She told the wide-eyed group of us who were sitting around her helping to shuck corn that we'd smell our favorite scent in the world when our mate was near, and if we were really fortunate, even before the mate bond was completed, we'd begin to have an almost telepathic connection, which would eventually evolve to a complete link that would allow us to communicate without words.

Since I've been around for quite some time now, and it had never happened to me or even any of my brothers, I always wondered if she was pulling the legs on a bunch of impressionable pups or not. Yet... my two favorite things to smell in the world are purple lilacs, and freshly cut grass, especially right after it rains.

I *know* she's the woman I helped yesterday, and her scent is even stronger today since I'm not wearing a mask and we were in each other's personal space, but don't know who I can ask to confirm my suspicions. Fuck. How can I keep her safe with all these people around? My wolf is clawing at my chest right now, wanting to spirit her away to his den.

"You alright, Brother?" Ogre asks, walking up next to me. "You seem a bit stunned."

Unwilling to share what I've just realized for myself, I shake my head, needing some time to wrap my head around this dazed discovery before sharing it with anyone, even my brothers. "Let's get inside and find out what Ms. Knight wants us to do for her attendees," I instruct.

As a group, the three of us find the event coordinator who is fluttering around finishing what appears to be a massive list of last-minute details. When she sees us, she smiles and holds out her hand to each of us as I introduce Ogre, Sly, and myself.

"How can we help?" I ask.

"Basically, just walk around and if a reader approaches or asks any questions, answer what you're able to, and be willing to pose for some pictures with them. This is all they've talked about in our reader's group since I announced we had members from some local clubs coming in," she replies.

"Sounds easy enough. How's the security?"

"Oh, we've got several undercover officers who'll be on the premises, so that's in order," she states.

My wolf isn't happy with her answer, but it's not like I can shift and tell her she's wrong. Instead, I just nod and smile. "We'll do what we can to ensure your attendees get what they came for today," I advise her, smirking.

Ogre's chuckle has me wanting to smack him; I know he's more interested in seeing if he can sneak in a little 'fun' with a willing participant, but since my mate is on the premises, I'm going to make sure he knows that's off the table until I've deemed she's safe and secure.

WE FIND A QUIET ALCOVE WHICH HAS BOTH OF MY brothers giving me a pointed look. Looking around, I lower my voice even though the likelihood of there being any other shifters here today is slim and none, and announce, "My mate is here."

"What the fuck?" Sly growls out. "Fuck, we need to call Fox and get the rest of the brothers here pronto!"

"No, I think we're good right now with just the three of us," I rebut. "Let's get a feel for everything and I'll point her out. She obviously doesn't know, so for the love of all that's holy, please be discreet." I glare at Ogre, who's known to blurt random shit out from time to time. "No need to scare her off before I've claimed her, you hear me?"

"Got it, Brother," they reply in unison.

"So, no sex in the back halls," Ogre mutters. "Fucking hell, that's one of the reasons I accepted this assignment." When I go to smack him, he smirks. "Just fucking with you, Chaos. No way in hell will I risk your mate."

"Appreciate it. Let's go check shit out then."

AFTER SPOTTING HER AND POINTING HER OUT TO both men, we split up with the understanding that if we see anything that needs attention, we'll use our pack's mental link. The downside to that is the rest of the club will be able to hear us, and of course, Fox could always make the call to show up, but right now, it's the best we can do because the noise level is insane, so phones are impossible to hear.

I'm standing near a table where several readers have somewhat cornered me, answering questions about what it's like being part of a club, when I spy her on the edge of the crowd. My wolf immediately perks up at her scent, her natural perfume invading my senses, and I have to fight for control so I don't push through the throng of crowded women to reach her. As the women start trickling off, she moves forward.

"Hi, um, I have a kind of weird question to ask if that's okay?" she stammers out, her face flushing.

Images flash through my mind of her whole body flushing after a night spent worshiping her, which I quickly push away.

"Go ahead, darlin'," I reply.

"Did you, were you the man who helped me change my tire yesterday?" she finally blurts, wringing her hands together.

"I am, but how did you figure out it was me?" I question, genuinely curious about her thought process. Of course, I want to know every single thing there is to know about her, and I will in due time.

"Well, I didn't think to tell you my name or even get yours, and although your face was covered, you're the only one here who somewhat resembles the biker who helped me yesterday."

"What do you mean?"

"You're the tallest biker here I've seen, and even with the mask on, I could tell you had a beard and figured it was the same color as your hair. Plus, your uh, ear gauges," she replies, her brows pinched, but her eyes never stray from mine, impressing me.

"The name's Chaos," I inform her, as I introduce myself I hold out my hand, eager to touch her and feel her skin flush against mine.

"Tressa," she says, tenderly placing her hand in mine.

The spark of recognition to my soul starts a frisson of something inside that I'm powerless to stop. She feels familiar, home-like, instead of the foreign feeling I get with strangers or other women I've met through the years. Immediately, her breathing settles so it matches and coincides with mine, and a subtle glow surrounds her, the aura tint wrapping her body like a shield. She appears to be shell shocked herself at the intense contact, but not in a bad way.

"Thank you, Chaos, for your help yesterday," she softly says, smiling up at me.

"Did you have any other problems with the spare after we parted ways?" I query.

"Not at all. Got to where I'm staying, and then ended up helping a few of the authors I create covers for set their tables up last night, after we ate dinner."

"You design covers?" That's intriguing, another crumb of information about her dropped, and it makes not only the wolf happy, but the man too.

"Yes, and I do some editing as well."

"Guess that means you can work anywhere then, huh?" My wolf barks in my head, not wanting to be left out of the excitement, he's twirling around inside of my head in triumph, wagging his tail as his tongue lolls, hanging out the side of his muzzle, drooling.

"She can work remotely," I insert, silently communicating with my wolf, sending him a mental grin as our souls fuse and preen with the aspect of what this means.

"As long as there's an internet connection, I'm good, yes," she teases, smiling. "Otherwise, I have to find someplace nearby that has Wi-Fi."

I make a mental note to check into the speed of our internet service because she'll have whatever she needs. While I want to stay here the rest of the day to talk with her, I see her cart is full and nearly overflowing, so I ask, "Are you leaving?"

She glances back at her abundant stack and giggles while shaking her head. "Um, no. I'm actually going to take these out to my car and store them, then come back in. I've already made two trips."

"Let me follow you out," I offer, not wanting to lose this easy banter we have flowing between us.

"That's not necessary."

Instinctively, I knew she was going to say something along these lines. She comes across as the type of woman who's humble and doesn't like to feel as if she's burdening anyone. She doesn't know this yet, but she's never going to be a hardship to me—as her mate, I long to take care of her and see to all of her needs, no matter how insignificant or pesky she feels they may be. It's an honor and a sacred privilege for a man to ensure his woman is carefree and satisfied in all aspects of her life. It's natural, instinctive, and ingrained into every strand of my DNA.

"Humor me, Tressa. Promise, I'm not a creeper, but a woman can never be too safe. If it makes you feel better, I'll just watch you go to your car, okay?"

While my wolf is clawing at me, unhappy about my decision not to follow her all the way to her car, I have to respect that she doesn't know about shifters or just how possessive we can be when we find our mates. Of course, I'm finding this out myself seeing as all I had to go on previously was what others said with regard to having a mate.

"Um, okay. Thanks."

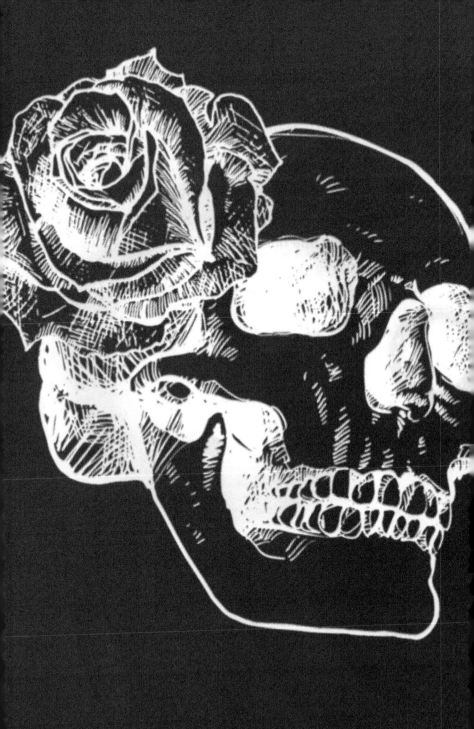

CHAPTER SEVEN

TRESSA

I'M HAVING AN ABSOLUTE BLAST, MEETING ALL THE authors who I didn't see last night, buying more books, and also talking to a lot of other readers as we wait in line or peruse the vast array of goodies, and not just books either, most have a variety of merchandise available to purchase as well. I grabbed hoodies for Nicole and myself, several book-related items, a sleeve for each of us to cover our e-readers with, and more swag than should be considered legal.

So, when I see the biker I crashed into earlier and take a closer look, I realize *he's* the man who helped me with my tire and head in his direction. I don't understand the feeling that washes over me watching him talk to the other women, especially when several ask for pictures with him, but it's definitely one I wish Nicole was here to discuss and help me decipher.

Because it almost feels like jealousy, only... how could that even be possible when I don't know his name, and our initial meeting was all of maybe twenty minutes? Except, that's exactly what I feel; a predatory sense of ownership encompasses me, I want to reach out and pull those women away from him, yelling that he's mine and yanking them out of this venue by the roots of their hair, like the old ladies do in the books I devour.

When I finally get the chance to speak, I manage to embarrass myself by stammering out my question. I'm used to people getting annoyed with me when that happens, and when he instead begins engaging me in a conversation, I'm shocked and discombobulated. He's acting as though he's interested.

In me.

Plain old Tressa Powers.

There's nothing special or spectacular about me. I keep my head down, work hard, and have dreams that will never come to fruition because I'm too damn shy to push myself outside of my comfort zone.

"I'll wait right here, Tressa," Chaos says, interrupting my inner dialogue as we reach the doors that will lead to the parking lot. I'm giddy when I see his shoulders stiffen, and his fingers dig into his palms. An understanding of how hard this is for a dominating man like him to stand back and let me walk the rest of the way alone to my car, unload my cart, and organize things wafts across my consciousness seeing his physical response.

"It won't take me long, I promise," I reply when I notice his jaw grind, hastening my pace and moving toward Ruby. Pulling my keys from my purse, I hit the key fob to open the back hatch, and when I get there, I begin to quickly unload all my stuff before closing and locking the doors. As I walk back toward him, his lazy smirk turns into a full smile, and I draw in a deep breath at how gorgeous he is, standing there so strong, menacing, and confident.

"Are you going back in right now?" he asks once I reach his side.

"I was going to take a quick break and grab a drink."

"Why don't you go sit over there and I'll get one for you?" he suggests, pointing to the seating area just outside the venue doors. Thankfully, there are a few places open, so I nod.

"But you don't need to get anything, I have drinks with me in my cooler," I protest, showing him my insulated bag while patting its side.

"I was going to grab myself a beer," he replies. "Figured you might want an adult beverage as well."

"Do you think they have frozen strawberry margaritas? They're my favorite," I question.

"I'm sure at a place like this they do," he advises. "Be right back."

I nod as I move over to the seating area, and he heads to one of the many bars I've seen. While I wait for him, I quickly send Nicole a text.

> Me: You're not going to believe this!

> Nini: What? Tell me!

> Me: The guy that helped me yesterday? He introduced himself after I asked him if he was the one who helped me or not.

> Nini: You were brave enough to approach him? Oh, you're growing up. I'm so proud.

> Me: Shut it, wench! Yeah, he had a bunch of women around him and hanging on his every word, this is going to sound strange, but it made me jealous, Nini!

> Nini: Holy crap. Love at first sight!

Me: Hardly. If you could see how gorgeous he is, you'd know better.

Nini: What have we talked about?

Me: I know, I know. But I'm telling you, there's no way a man like him, looking the way he does, would want someone like me.

Nini: You mean a kind, generous, beautiful soul? He'd be a fool if he didn't!

Me: Gotta go. He went to get us a drink so I could take a break and he's walking toward me now.

Nini: FULL DETAILS TONIGHT!

Me: Yes, ma'am!

"Here you go, Tressa," he says, handing me the biggest frozen margarita I've ever seen. "I wasn't sure, so I had them rim it with sugar."

"That's perfect," I reply, taking a sip. "Oh, this is luscious."

He chuckles, causing me to blush. "Glad you like it."

"Did you come with anyone else from your club?" I ask, suddenly wanting to know everything there is about him. "And I know you probably won't tell me, but I'm pretty sure Chaos isn't your legal name."

His chuckles turn into laughter, causing several folks who are wandering around to glance in our direction. "Haven't used that in so long, I'd probably have to look it up."

"But what about work and stuff?" I inquire.

"Club owns several businesses, so I'm positive all the legal bullshit is filed underneath my government issued name, but all of us go by our road names, darlin'," he answers, taking a long pull from his beer.

I giggle, picturing his bank debit card with 'Chaos' on it then nearly choke on the swallow I just took of my drink when he raises his brow at me, smirking as if he knows what I'm thinking. "What?" I ask, trying to act innocent.

"I don't deal with banks, Tressa, they're a pain in the ass. So no, there's no debit card floating around out there with Chaos stamped on it."

Wait. I didn't say that out loud. How did he know what I was thinking? When I glance at him, my eyes wide, he winks. Instead of asking him another question, I decide to keep my confusion to myself and finish my drink.

"You ready to head back inside?" he asks when I have just a few sips left. When I nod, he places my glass and his empty beer on the side table, then helps me to my feet. Leaning in, he whispers, "I promise, I'll explain what just happened later. Hoping you'll agree to go to dinner with me once this is all over."

"I... I think I'd like that," I stutter, causing him to grin at me. My insides flutter and I feel like I've been lit up inside with a whole bunch of shooting fireworks. For the first time in my life, I feel like I'm wanted, and not in just a sexual way. He seems interested in everything I say, but I'm the same way; I want to know it all.

"Good, then it's a plan. Now, I have to go find my brothers and make sure they're not getting into any shit. We'll meet up when it's all over, okay?"

"Okay."

He strides off in a different direction from me as I head back to the area where I left off before I had to empty out my cart. As I stand in the next line, my mind is feverishly working overtime, because shit like what's happened today simply does not happen to me.

Ever.

CHAPTER EIGHT

CHAOS

JUST THE SMALL BIT OF CONTACT WITH TRESSA HAS temporarily satisfied my wolf, which is a good thing, because we've got about two more hours of this absolute insanity before I can talk to her again. Ogre walks over and asks, "Everything good, Brother?"

"Definitely. She's willing to do dinner tonight."

"You going to tell her?"

"Don't really have a choice, do I?"

"No, but hell, none of us have experience in this area. What if she freaks out?" It's a valid question, but not one I can afford to get stuck on. Whatever happens, however she reacts, I'll have to deal with it when it comes. My genetic anomaly isn't something I can hide; my wolf is a part of me and he's never going away.

But I have faith in fate. She'd never have been exposed to me by the higher ups if she wasn't capable of handling my secret.

"She seems to be pretty sensible," Ogre says.

"Quiet, though," Sly remarks, walking up to us. When I glare at him, he puts his hands up. "Just saying, Chaos, that she's what my nana called a quiet pretty. She's not flashy and all in your face, and her beauty shines from the inside out. She's the kind of woman who gets overlooked for that very reason, I'm sure."

"She's pretty shy from what I've observed," I reply. "Very apologetic if she feels she overstepped, that kind of thing."

That's the benefit of shifter hearing; I may not have been in her direct proximity, but can pinpoint her voice in this room despite the booming noise. I smirk when I remember the visual I got through our newly formed bond; what she doesn't realize is once I claim her, not only will our connection fully snap into place, but she'll become a shifter as well.

"I suspect that'll change once she's around all of us," Ogre jests, snickering.

I hear her mumbling about needing to go back out to Ruby, which must be her car, only the beers I've been continuously drinking finally need to be expelled.

"Fuck, I need to take a leak. Ogre, she's heading out to her car, go keep an eye on her and I'll be there as soon as I can," I growl out, stomping toward the exit so I can hit the head and relieve my bladder.

I'm walking toward where I know she's parked so I can hopefully talk to her again when I hear Ogre in my head and my pace hastens and my steps get larger.

"Chaos, call Fox, get the guys here quick. They took her. I'm following." Ogre's tone is harsh, I can hear the distress and guilt woven into his words.

"Who took her?" I bellow through our link.

"Fucking Bastians, Brother. She was turning to come back inside when a white van pulled up and they jerked her inside then took off."

"How do you know it was the Bastians?" Fox's calm voice does nothing to defray the rage fueling me right now. Nor am I surprised that he saved me a phone call, because right now, my focus is on finding her and rescuing her from the absolute scum of the earth fuckers. There's no telling what they'll do to her if we don't get to her before they bunk down somewhere with her. More than likely, they won't go

to their clubhouse, but nobody has ever claimed they have brains. The way they operate, they'll find some low-key motel or ambush some unsuspecting family and take over their homestead.

I get blindsided by rage.

Rage that will consume me, and have me shifting, scaring a shit ton of humans if I don't get it under control and put a leash on it.

Rage that already has me mentally dismembering each and every person in that despicable, vile excuse for a club. By the time I'm done with them, there won't be anything left of their bodies to identify.

"Saw the cut, Pres."

My wolf internally howls, much like I would do if it wouldn't scare the countless humans who are around right now.

Soon, I promise.

ONCE ON MY BIKE WITH MY BLUETOOTH ON, WHICH will make it a lot easier to focus, I find that Popeye has already sent the coordinates of the Bastian's clubhouse to my GPS, and I grin. No clue how that fucker is able to do half the shit he does, but if it means I can find my mate and save her from whatever nefarious things those bastards have planned, I'm good. I was wrong in my assessment earlier; they *are* crazy enough to take Tressa to their club. Most likely, that's because they figured we wouldn't be able to track them and crack the code that pinpoints their location. Hidden doesn't mean it can't be found, it just makes it more tedious to do.

And we have a weapon in our arsenal. Thank fuck Popeye is part of our team and not an adversary.

"Anything?" I probe when silence pervades the line. I'm trying to avoid losing my shit, but my wolf is to the point he wants to take over and force the shift. The last time he tried that, when I was far younger and not as in control, it didn't end up too well for my bike, so other than my vision sharpening, some extra hair sprouting on my arms, and my deeper voice, I'm keeping a tight rein on the bastard.

Because I *will* lose my shit and go chaotic once I get where I'm supposed to be; it's how I earned my road name all those years ago.

"They appear to be heading to their clubhouse. Rest of the brothers are on the way, Fox said to pull off about a mile before it, behind Filler Up, a closed-down gas station. I'm monitoring from here," Popeye advises. "Bring her home safe and sound, Brother. We got you."

I don't bother answering; my mind is on the diminutive pixie who has captivated me since I saw her stranded on the side of the road. Then, finding out she's my mate? I'm thoroughly entranced even knowing that what I'll be telling her about me, and our situation could go sideways. My wolf, however, does not give a fuck. He's already planning the 'new den' we're going to build on the club property, so we're not surrounded by everyone else and have some privacy as we get to know each other and start our lives.

***

"I'M NOT WAITING ANY LONGER, PRES," I GROWL OUT, my wolf's eyes glaring at my president as he informs us of how things are going to go down. "You know what they do to women, and how they treat them! She's my fucking *mate* and there's no way in hell I'll let her endure even a minute of fear over what they're probably already taunting her with!"

"We go under the cover of darkness, Chaos," he bites out, giving me his own glare, which would have a lesser shifter cowering. Unfortunately for him, for everyone actually, I come from a longass line of alpha shifters, so I'm completely unphased by his attempt.

"By then she could be dead," I bellow, my fists clenched.

"She's not dead," Popeye asserts through our mental link. *"Got a drone flying over their clubhouse now and have a visual on her through a window. She's still breathing."*

That does little to calm me or my wolf. Despite my impeccable control, I'm fighting a total shift but keep watching as fur ripples up and down my arms each time I flex them.

"Like I said, I'm not waiting until dark, *Pres*," I sneer, my wolf peering at him as my canines elongate.

"Pres, he could shift and check things out, get the lay of the land. There are a ton of trees and shit to camouflage him, and from what I've seen on the drone, half of them are drunk off their asses, and the other half look like they're smoking a little green," Popeye advises through our link.

Without waiting for anyone else, I remove my cut and tuck it into my saddlebags, then quickly undress before shifting into my auburn wolf. Throwing my head back, I howl out my animosity and frustration, then quickly lope off in the direction of the clubhouse, my intent purposeful as I hone in on my mate's aromatic scent.

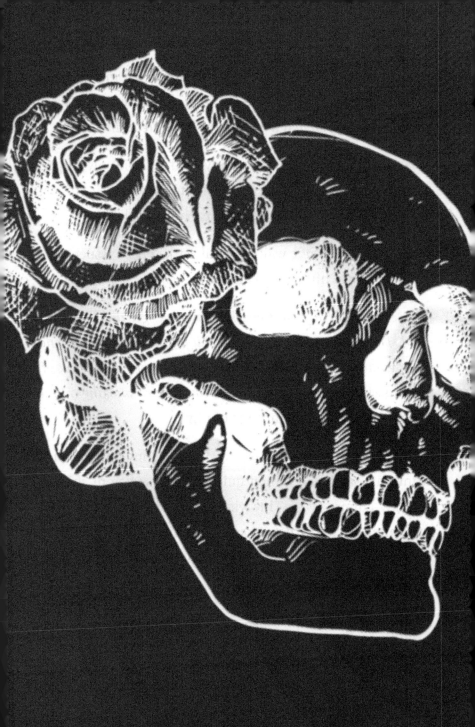

CHAPTER NINE

TRESSA

"COME ON, THINK TRESSA," I MUTTER TO MYSELF. I woke up to find myself trussed up like a Thanksgiving turkey. Of course, if I hadn't gotten a streak of bravery and mouthed off at the jerks who took me, I probably wouldn't have taken the blow to my face that knocked me out.

Newsflash, getting hit like that hurts! My face feels puffy, and one eye is partially closed, while I can taste blood in my mouth. Swiping my tongue over my lips, I wince when I feel the split.

"That's gonna leave a mark," I whisper, feverishly trying to get my hands loose from their bindings. I momentarily feel like I'm succeeding until fire races up my arms and I realize I've managed to rip the skin open at my wrists. "Dammit. What do all the heroines in the books I read do when they find themselves kidnapped? Because I *know* these guys aren't going to let me go, at least not still alive. I may not be worldly, but I'm not naive nor stupid."

Their comments have also let me know what they're planning for me and it's the stuff nightmares are made of, which says a lot coming from a self-confessed crime junkie. The tall guy with greasy, gray hair tied back with a piece of leather, whose cut denotes he's the president of this band of miscreants, has already stated rather loudly that he's first in line once the party really gets going. I had to read between the lines, but quickly realized that I'm the party favor they intend to play with. Now, I've always admired the old ladies who've finagled their way to freedom after being unwillingly taken. I even admire their tenacity for waiting to be rescued, but I don't want to be that woman. In my mind, these scenes weren't so gut wrenching, but in real life, it's harrowing.

Shudders wrack my body at the thought of any of them touching me in any way, much less like *that*. I'd rather try and throw myself backward onto the floor and hope I break my neck or something than allow them to violate me.

Hearing a noise at the door, I look up and see one of the guys who took me leering at me before he throws his head back and cackles. "Time's almost up, pretty lady. Once we're done with you, there won't be anything left for the vultures to snack on."

One single tear rolls down my face before I can control myself. Seeing it, he laughs menacingly, and pulls out a knife from a sheath at his waist, walking toward me.

I'm sorry, Nini, that I won't get to tell you about my brief time with the handsome biker. Right now, though, I'm so glad you didn't come with me and you're not here to experience this torment.

WAKING UP, AGAIN, I FEEL REALLY DISORIENTED until reality returns and my body is overcome with the shakes. I can feel the blood running down my face, chest, arms, and legs. Emotions swamp me and I send up a silent prayer either to be rescued, which is highly unlikely since no one knows I'm gone, or to bleed out before I'm molested.

My left shoulder is burning, and I carefully look down to see what appears to be a stab wound near the crease of my armpit. A small cry erupts as the memories flood in while flames of pain crash through my body.

"Ah, now little girlie, don't be sad. We're going to show you a good time," he jeered while smirking at me and juggling his knife from hand to hand.

I probably would've been just fine, but as he leaned down into my personal space and tried to lick my cheek, I reared back as revulsion caused me to slightly gag. His body odor was unpleasant, and with his entrance, a pungent aroma began to fill the small space, and it made me want to plug my nose, but it was the hot, fetid breath that I breathed in that had me realizing I wasn't going to survive anything they did to me.

In anger from my reaction to his all-around stench, he retaliated and struck out, his knife slicing across my cheek, fileting it open, before he started mixing up his attack by stabbing and punching me, switching from one form of punishment to the other. I'm quite certain he would've killed me, but another member appeared, saw what he was doing, and yelled at him to stop. I almost thought he was my savior until he continued speaking, upset that he was going to end me before they were able to use and abuse me. Stepping back, he grinned maliciously before bringing the knife to his mouth and licking my blood, cleaning the blade.

Mercifully, I passed out as he left the room, but not before I overheard them sharing, comparing their ideas of how to make me scream the loudest.

WHICH LEADS ME TO NOW. AS I TRY TO IGNORE THE persistent dripping noise from my life's fluid hitting the floor, I gaze toward where whatever noise I heard while unconscious came from, only to see intelligent, whiskey-brown eyes staring at me through the filthy window.

What I see has me questioning if I'm awake or still lost in the land of sleep. A wolf? Do they even live in this part of the country? Shaking my head, this has convinced me that I'm already dead. I continue to look at the beautiful specimen who has appeared, admiring his caramel-colored pelt.

"I wish this was one of my shifter books, because that would mean you're going to rescue me, and save me from certain death," I mumble as tremors overtake my body. I suspect I'm going into shock from the abundant blood loss, but there's nothing I can do. I can't staunch it by wrapping it to stop the heavy flow since I'm tied to a chair.

"Calm, little mate, I'll have you out of there soon," a voice whispers in my head.

A small smile escapes, not because the imaginary wolf is talking to me in my head, but because I know that my pain and suffering is fixing to end. I must be on the brink of death if I'm not dead already.

"I obviously hit my head harder than I thought. Either that, or it was the beating they gave me," I utter, my voice slightly louder since the music pounding from outside the room is so loud, I doubt anyone can hear me. Because shifters don't exist in real life. They're a myth, a product of an author's mind, and while the thought of having someone who was a combination of a person and a magnificent animal, or hell even a vampire if they existed, is great, I remind myself that it's just fiction.

Sighing, I give a slight nod as the wolf dips its head. When in Rome, live as the Romans do, they say. If my mind wants to conjure a wolf shifter to comfort me during my last moments on earth, who am I to argue? It's a fantasy I don't mind experiencing before drawing my final breath. When he throws his head back and howls, chills of fear race down my spine. I can *feel* his intent to decimate and destroy everyone who is inside this place and that amount of fury scares the hell out of me.

Because what if they get to me before he does?

"Mate, never doubt my devotion to you. Calm yourself, this will be over soon."

Feeling the darkness trying to pull me under once again, I give the wolf a sad smile. As my vision goes black, my thoughts are on the tall, handsome biker I met just a few, short hours ago. Guess I'll be missing dinner with him as well.

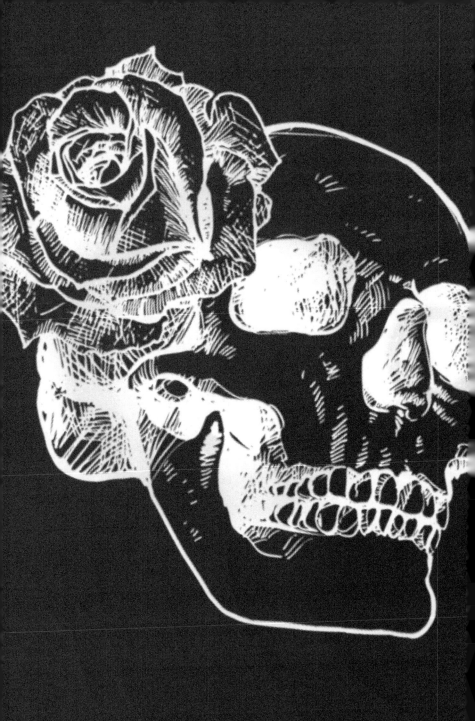

CHAPTER TEN

CHAOS

IT DOESN'T TAKE ME LONG TO FIND THE BASTIANS' clubhouse, and I stick to the shadows as I move around until Tressa's scent is so strong, I know she's on the other side of this building's wall from me. Nothing more than tar and mortar keeps us apart, but the foundation is not sturdy enough to withstand my wolf when he's gone nuclear, and it won't keep me from tearing it apart, brick by brick, if that's what it takes for me to get to her. While I'd love nothing more than to crash through the front door and begin shredding every single person in my sight, I need to figure out how many of these lowlifes are actually inside. I'm not worried about doing it on my own; I know my brothers are already on their way to help. No man is ever left behind, the military isn't the only group of soldiers that's adopted that noble motto. Wolves and bikers live by it too.

But she's *my* mate, and as such, I need to be the one to assess how badly she may be hurt so I can evaluate the situation and formulate a plan of action. When I peer through the dirty, cracked window, the angry howl I emit comes bubbling out of my chest. It's full of sorrow, rage, angst; every emotion that has gone through me since hearing of her kidnapping is roared into the air, although I'm unworried about the fuckers inside hearing my bellowing howl because the thumping of the bass from their music echoes to the outside. The ground vibrates underneath my paws from the level of their radio.

"She's hurt, bad," I report to my brothers through our link.

"We're almost there," Fox advises.

"There's blood everywhere," I retort, apprising them of the situation.

"Soon there'll be more bloodshed," Stealth replies, his tone deadly and imminent.

As our SAA, or Sergeant-at-Arms, he's one big fucker in his human form, with muscles bulging on top of muscles. However, when he shifts, he's humongous. As shifters, we're all genetically bigger than the average wolf, but it's as if he has a bit more of something mixed in, because he's almost as big as a dire wolf. Regardless, with him at my side, we're going to be painting the insides of this piece of shit place crimson.

Blood will flow from every single fucker who dared to lay a finger on and touched my mate. And the ones who didn't? Well, we know this club's proclivities, so they're not without any blame, and due to their association with the others, they *will* suffer the same fate.

I'M STILL STARING THROUGH THE SLUDGE COVERED window at her, while I await my brothers, when she stirs, likely because she was roused from my howl.

"I wish this was one of my shifter books, because that would mean you're going to rescue me, and save me from certain death," she mumbles as she starts shaking. Her convulsions are hard, causing the blood to flow faster.

Hurry the fuck up, I think. *I'm about to lose my shit.* I don't bother saying anything through the link with my brothers; I'm sure the fact I shifted and took off let them know I was teetering on the edge.

Hoping to help her, I say through our link, *"Calm, little mate, I'll have you out of there soon."*

"I obviously hit my head harder than I thought. Either that, or it was the beating they gave me," she states, unaware that I understand every word she's saying. And with each one she speaks, I become more enraged.

She nods at me, so I dip my head before throwing my head back and howling once more. I can feel her fear, it's nearly palpable, and hear her worrying about them getting her before I can save her.

"Mate, never doubt my devotion to you. Calm yourself, this will be over soon."

When she passes out once more, I make a quick tour around the house and count at least ten men present. It doesn't mean there aren't more in a room that has no windows, but if memory serves from the intel Popeye has been continuously feeding us through our link, they only have ten to twelve members all together. It's ironic, though, because for being such a small club, they wreak havoc in every way possible.

Drugs? They manufacture, sell, and even distribute them, and not just weed. Lately, they've been lacing their product with fentanyl, and people, mostly teenagers, are dying from the overdose. It's something we as a club are working to eradicate. While we'll probably send the information to the authorities as soon as we're sure we've got all the main players identified, it's still possible we'll inflict a little brand of our own type of justice.

Trafficking? The number of young girls and boys who have come up missing in and around Zephyr Hills, has tripled over the past six months. Popeye was able to access some site on the dark web and followed the thread, finding most of them. Sadly, the ones he found had been sold, and two of them were bought by a sick fucker who enjoys making snuff films, so the likelihood they're still breathing is slim and none. Popeye has a lead he's been following to find that guy because he's going down. CannibalLechter, the screen name that keeps popping up, and which is obviously this fucker's attempt to say he's like that character, Hannibal Lechter, from the movies, is his screen name and even though he's pretty good at hiding behind what Popeye says are proxy servers, my brother is better.

Hell, he's been hired by several different government officials for jobs that range from finding hidden monies nestled away in offshore accounts by corrupt politicians, to tracking down missing children. He's even assisted in helping to solve some cold cases, although his name will never be mentioned because he sends the information he digs up to a contact he's made in the FBI.

Women and children, which most who have taken would be classified as, are sacrosanct to our kind. We protect them, cherish them, and will fight to the death to ensure they don't suffer any harm. When it comes to a mate, however, we're what I'm sure some folks would deem as over the top. They're heavily guarded, especially once they are carrying pups, and while they're not stifled with respect to living their lives, we make it our number one priority to ensure they always breathe easy. I remember growing up in my father's pack how he was with my mother. She knew when she went into town to the farmer's market there was someone overseeing her, but wasn't upset by that fact. No, when I asked her once, she told me she knew it meant she could go about her business while my dad or whoever was with her that day, ensured no danger touched her.

I'M BACK AT THE WINDOW KEEPING MY EYE ON Tressa when the door opens, and I see a dead man walking come inside, a gleam in his eyes I don't particularly care for as he toys with a knife in his hands. Instinctively, I know he's the one who caused her to bleed so profusely, and I vow his death will be painful.

Every inch of skin will be peeled from his body, and if he passes out, we'll wake him back up. His dick will be cut off and shoved down his throat, then I'll use my claws which are far sharper than any blade known to mankind, and inflict the same wounds on him that he did to her.

When he approaches her to see her passed out, he clicks his tongue and I hear him say, "Little girl, it's time to wake up and party."

Red fills my vision as I spring into action, busting through the flimsy window as if it were Saran wrap and not glass. As shards fall around me, I waste no time leaping on him and tackling him to the ground, the knife skittering away.

"You starting the party without me?" Stealth asks, humor in his tone.

"Yes, they were about to drag her out of the room and 'party' with her," I growl out, barely managing to stop from ripping the bastard's throat out.

Once I'm sure he's subdued, and won't be waking up any time soon, I slip through the opened door and prowl down the hallway.

It's time for me to play. This has now become my party.

———

"WHAT THE FUCK?" AS I LEAP UP AND SWIPE MY PAW through the fucker's throat, I imagine him saying that very same thing when he's ushered through the gates of Hell.

Continuing on my path of destruction, I move down the hallway further and into what is apparently the club's common room. Kind of stupid if you ask me because the whole front is glass-plated, and I doubt these idiots are intelligent enough to have replaced it with bullet-proof glass. Evidence of their so-called partying is everywhere; empty beer and liquor bottles litter the tables, with drugs and the associated paraphernalia lying around as well. I'm able to move through them without anyone saying anything until I catch a brief whiff of Tressa.

Glaring straight ahead, I spot a beefy male who has busted knuckles and I know he's one of the ones who beat her. It doesn't matter because eventually, each of these assholes are going to pay in blood. He happens to glance in my direction and his eyes widen.

"Who let the ugly fucking dog inside?" he bellows, pulling out a gun.

As he pulls the trigger, I leap for him, my paws and claws extended, raking down his body from his shoulders to his gut, flaying him open. He sucks in a harsh breath while looking down at his intestines which are now tumbling out of his shredded shirt before he falls forward, dead, which finally elicits a somewhat delayed reaction from the rest of the men sitting around. Guns are drawn and bullets start to fly when suddenly, the glass shatters and Fox, Stealth, Ogre, and Sly come bounding through, jaws gnashing as they each pounce on one of the bikers rushing us. I feel a slight sting and shake it off, uncaring whether it's from the flying glass or a stray bullet.

Because truthfully, short of them lopping off my head or removing my heart, I'm damn near immortal. No, I won't live forever because I'm not a god or a vampire, but as a shifter, I'll be around for a long time. A feral grin covers my face, blood dripping from my canines and paws as I track down the next victim. Eradicating the Bastians probably won't stop all the shit that's been happening in our area, but I suspect it might slow some of it down, giving Popeye a chance to find out more intel and maybe even save a few lives in the process.

"Go check on your mate, we've got the rest of them," Fox orders.

He doesn't have to tell me twice. I may have jumped the gun on this little party, and I may catch shit for it later, which I'll gladly accept, but for the most part, I listen to my president and when he issues a decree, I follow it. Running back down the hallway to the room where she's being kept, I can't hold in the whine that emits from me; seeing her slumped in the chair shreds me.

I nuzzle her while taking note that her skin is alarmingly gray, her wounds are still bleeding, and she's unconscious. Her heartbeat is faint and slow, another concern. While I debate the best course of action, I see her unswollen eye flutter open then widen when she catches a glimpse of me by her side. When I feel her fingers, which have to be almost numb by now, lightly stroke my haunch, I whine again. She smiles, splitting her lip open again, and says, "Thank you for saving me," before she sinks back into unconsciousness, blood once again flowing down her ravaged face.

BY THE TIME MY BROTHERS ENTER THE ROOM, SOME still in their shifted form while Ogre and one of the prospects appear fully clothed, I've managed to undo her bindings, shift, and am holding her cradled in my arms. The sheer level of protectiveness that has come over me has me growling at my brothers as they breach the doorway.

Fox's hands go up and he calmly states, "Ogre brought your clothes, Chaos, and the prospect has a blanket for you to wrap around your mate. Don't think she'd understand why you're holding her while naked."

His soothing tone, which is unlike him most of the time, breaks through the frenzied thoughts that've been assaulting me since finding her such a short time ago. I stand with her in my arms, and watch the prospect open the blanket and place it on the dirty concrete, away from the pool of blood thankfully, so I can lay her down then quickly dress.

"That sonofabitch," I insinuate, pointing to the still-unconscious biker, "needs to go back to the 'house."

"Prospect, take him to the van. We got your bike here too, Brother, but thinking you're not going to let her go, are you?" Fox asks, smirking at me.

Fucker.

As crazed as I am right now, fucking with me isn't a good idea. With a glare, I gently wrap Tressa in the blanket then pick her back up. "Let the prospect get it back."

Normally, I don't want anyone else riding my girl, but I also don't want to let my mate out of my arms, much less my sight. As we leave the house, I see Stealth setting down explosives. Immediately, I know they're going to demolish this pit and erase any evidence of our involvement with multiple deaths.

It takes a few minutes to get settled in the van and my concern grows when she doesn't utter so much as a moan. I'm trying not to lose my shit again, and yell for everyone to hurry because I know my brothers; they're working as quickly as possible to get us out of here and me back to the clubhouse so Doc can check Tressa out.

HALFWAY TO THE CLUBHOUSE, STEALTH LOOKS AT ME through the rearview mirror, and says, "You need to just go ahead and do it, Brother. She's fading."

He chose to let the others figure out how to get our bikes back so he could drive. No one I'd rather have with me to be honest, simply because when it comes to protecting and defending, he's almost as crazy as I am.

I sigh, then nod. "Kinda feels wrong, though, because she has no clue shifters really exist. She only believes they live through her books."

"Well, think of it this way. If you *don't* do it, Doc won't have anything to examine because she'll be fucking dead," he retorts, being blunt as always, never pulling any punches. "Otherwise, you could let Doc do his thing which wouldn't impact the mate bond so she'd heal. This way, however, you'll have another tie to her."

Fuck. For someone who is normally decisive, I feel out of sorts and wishy washy. Deciding I won't lose my mate over my concerns, and will ask for forgiveness later if that's what I have to do, I lift her arm and bring her wrist to my mouth. Elongating my canines, I pierce my own lip then puncture her skin, allowing my blood to drip inside the two prick marks before I encase the small wound with my mouth, and push my own saliva, which has healing properties that will help rehabilitate her body and knit her flesh back together, into her battered flesh.

I lose track of time until I can physically sense her heartbeat strengthening. Pulling back, I lick the wound to seal it and cradle her close, needing to feel her skin warming as her cells start to regenerate. Already, her pallor has decreased and even though she's still knocked out, she seems to be resting easier.

"That's gonna add another layer to our bond," I muse, forgetting momentarily that Stealth is driving.

"Which isn't a bad thing, Brother," he taunts. "You're already a goner over this woman and she hasn't got the first fucking clue that shifters exist, mates are real, or that she's yours. Gonna be fun times around the 'house, huh?"

"Fucker," I grumble, causing him to burst into laughter.

THERE WAS A BIT OF A STRUGGLE WHEN WE GOT BACK to the clubhouse. I wasn't willing to let her go, but couldn't safely get out of the vehicle, either. It wasn't until Stealth stood inside the opened door and held his arms out that I was able to transfer her to him. No clue why, except for our closeness, because Fox, Sly, and even Ogre had tried and been rebuffed. I know I'll catch some shit for my behavior, but I've got a long memory and if any of them give me any snarky commentary, I'll tuck it away for when they find their own damn mate.

Payback's a bitch and all that shit.

Even harder was allowing so many into my room, which my wolf deemed his den long ago, especially once she is placed on my king-size bed. The chuckles from my brothers over my growls is giving me a headache, and finally taking pity on me, Fox orders everyone out.

Turning to go, he says, "Doc's on his way. I can tell you did what you had to do because honestly, Brother, I expected her to be dead before we got here. Sending Ogre and Sly over to the hotel she was staying at to get her stuff, and also back to the event venue to bring her vehicle here. The less questions, the better, you know?"

Thankfully, one of the guys found her purse with her keys, phone, and other shit in it, forgotten in the van she was kidnapped in, which is how they're taking care of those things now.

"Appreciate it, Brother," I reply, my gaze never leaving her face. She looks like she's sleeping now, and I've been watching the slow, minute healing going on with total fascination.

I mean, as shifters, we heal quickly, but I'm impressed that already, the bruising has lightened significantly, and some of the smaller cuts and gashes have knit themselves together. If she keeps this up, Doc's exam will be more cursory than anything.

Once he leaves, I get up and head into the bathroom to wet a cloth and try to clean her up. On my way back, I hear a light knock on my door. Upon opening it, I see Renda standing there, her eyes downcast although her arms are weighed down with towels, a bowl, and a bar of soap.

"Renda? What do you need?" I try to soften my voice because she looks very nervous, but it must not work well because she yelps slightly, then blushes.

"Um, I heard your mate was hurt and thought you might need stuff to clean her up while you wait for Doc," she finally manages to stammer. "I wasn't eavesdropping, Chaos, I swear!"

"Didn't think you were, Renda. Yes, she's my mate, and she's injured, so I appreciate you thinking to do this," I reply, taking the items from her trembling arms. "She doesn't know about this life, or shifters, or anything. Make sure the other girls realize if they fuck around with her once she's on her feet again, they'll find out how I earned my road name."

"Absolutely, Chaos. We all got together, and already talked about it, and we're excited for you, actually."

While I'm not exactly happy that the club girls are talking about me, at least they're not trying to ride my dick, and it appears they're willing to help my mate assimilate into our world. Shaking my head at the absurdity of this current conversation, I merely nod, and step back from the door, hoping she takes the hint.

"Appreciate the stuff."

"Sure, no problem. Um, if you need anything else, let me know and I'll get it for you," she says.

Instead of answering, I close the door and head back into the bathroom. As the bowl fills with warm water, I unwrap the bar of soap, smirking. It's an antibacterial soap or some shit, but is unscented, which is probably not a bad thing considering all the slices Tressa has covering her body. The last thing I want to do is cause her any kind of pain. Returning to her side, I place the bowl on the nightstand and look down, only to see her beautiful eyes staring up at me.

"Chaos? Am I dead? Or dreaming?" she whispers. Her throat sounds raw, and I fight back the anger that rushes through me, thinking of the reason why she would have a sore throat. I don't see any marks on her neck, so that means whether she was aware of it or not, she screamed during their torture of her.

I wish they weren't all dead so I could hurt them again. Then I remember one of them *is* left, cooling his heels in our interrogation room. Smirking, I let my mind drift a bit about everything I plan to do to him before he draws his last breath.

"Neither, darlin'," I reply. "What do you remember?"

"A bunch of things that don't make a lot of sense, to be honest," she croaks out. "Can you tell me?"

Clearing my throat, I lean in and swipe the hair from her face. "You got kidnapped at the signing, Tressa. One of my brothers, Ogre, saw them take you and followed behind while letting the rest of us know where you were. I'm sorry, little one, that you were hurt. We got to you as soon as we could."

"They didn't... they didn't rape me or anything," she murmurs, her face flushing bright red as her eyes look anywhere but at me.

"Wouldn't have made a difference to me, sweetheart."

"What do you mean?" she asks, her gaze finally meeting mine once again.

"You're my mate."

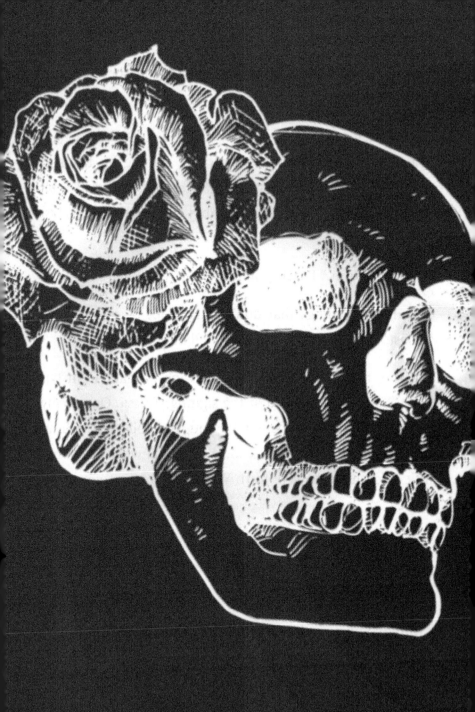

CHAPTER ELEVEN

Tressa

"You're my mate."

At his words, I start laughing hysterically, because mates aren't real. They're fiction.

"There's no such thing, Chaos. Now I know I'm either in a coma or dead. Which would suck because Nini wanted me to dish out all of the details of our dinner when I talk to her later on. Shit, does Nini know I died?" I ramble on and on, growing increasingly agitated just thinking about my best friend worrying over what might have happened when she doesn't hear from me.

"Tressa, little mate, look at me," he commands. His voice is delicious when he's speaking, but when he adds that little extra *oomph*, I feel it in every pore of my body. Even more incredulous to my reeling mind is I've heard that phrase before, in the place I was being held. Despite the craziness of the situation, hearing it settles me slightly, and I feel a calm rush over me.

Speaking of, I glance down and see my blood-soaked T-shirt practically shredded, but obviously stuck to me. Looking to my left at where the stab wound was, I notice it's stopped bleeding but don't know if it's because the fabric stopped it, or if there's something else. I know my eye that was swollen shut is now slightly opened, which is weird, because earlier, I couldn't have pried it open with a toothpick. Blinking experimentally, I realize there's not as much pain in that area either, so I raise my arms to look at my wrecked wrists, only to see skin that looks like it's nearly healed.

"What the hell is going on?" I murmur, turning them back and forth. "How long have I been out? There's no way I am nearly healed, I felt my arms burning when the skin tore after I tried to break the bindings! Plus, everything *hurt*, Chaos, and now, I just ache. I don't understand."

Now frustrated, I feel the tears come to my eyes and slip down my cheeks. He tries to catch them, but they're flowing too fast, and he gives up, reaching next to him to grab a cloth which he puts in a bowl, wrings out, then places against my face, gently wiping away the tears and blood.

"What's going on is something I know you think is fiction. You're not dead. You weren't in a coma for weeks or even months," he growls out. "We don't share this with anyone, unless it's a need to know."

"And I guess I need to know?" I sass. I have no clue when my backbone decided to show up, because the last time it did, I paid the price with a black eye and busted lip.

"You do."

"So, enlighten me. Wait, let me ask you something first. Did... did I really see a wolf earlier, or was that a hallucination?"

He smirks, and I watch in awe as his hand turns into a paw with razor-sharp claws, while his eyes change, and I find myself staring into the whiskey-colored orbs I saw earlier.

"No. No fucking way," I whisper. "Shifters are real?"

"We're real, darlin', and I've got a bigger newsflash for you, you're going to be one as well."

Wait a minute. I *heard* what he said quite clearly, but his lips never moved. At this realization, I guess the excitement combined with everything from before is too much because I find myself falling into the abyss once again.

WHEN I WAKE UP AGAIN, IT'S TO FIND A STRANGER peering at me. "Hello, Tressa, my name is Doc, and I want to check you over and see if you need any stitches, although from the looks of things, it probably won't be necessary at all."

"Hello," I rasp out, my throat now so dry that combined with my screaming earlier, I feel like a blowtorch has been used on me.

"Do you need something to drink?" he kindly asks.

When I nod, he brings a cup to me and as I struggle to sit up, I feel two strong arms band around me and set me against the headboard. Once a pillow is placed behind my head, the arms are removed, and I feel him settle against my side.

Him.

Chaos.

My brain is still reeling over what he told me earlier as I sip on the water until Doc pulls the cup away. "Not too much until I'm sure there's no internal damage we need to be concerned about," he advises.

The growl that reverberates through the room has me looking toward the man who is larger than life, at least to me. Despite the fact he's reclining in the bed, I can feel the tension coiled within him, especially each time Doc comes near me. For whatever reason, I reach out and place my hand on top of his, then squeal when he laces his fingers through mine.

"Mine. Mine to protect. To cherish. To love."

Again, I hear him, but not out loud. How is this possible?

"Because our bond is being formed and growing stronger. Once we have sex and complete the mating, it will fully snap into place."

"Really?" I ask, which has Doc looking at me strangely. "What? I'm hearing him in my head, dammit, and I don't understand how it's possible!"

Doc crouches next to me and takes my hand in his. "So, I understand you're just learning about our kind. When Chaos bit you earlier to save your life, it started the process since you're his mate. Eventually, you'll be able to talk to him in your mind and respond when he speaks. Right now, since the bond is incomplete until you have sex, you can only hear what he has to say."

Sex. Just the thought of this gorgeous man looking at my naked body is a bit scary. I'm curvy, but not fat. However, I have a slight pooch from those late-night gab sessions with Nini that won't go anywhere despite my best intentions. But when I imagine his hands, mouth, and tongue on me? I can feel the blood rush to my face and know I look like a ripe tomato. I can't even fathom the rest of it; I will probably faint again which kind of pisses me off. I swear I've never passed out as often as I have today. Chaos will think I'm a wimp.

"My mate is strong and courageous," he whispers next to my ear, his hand squeezing mine. When I look at him, he winks, which sends a rush of desire to my core.

Yeah, I'm in trouble. I'm not a virgin, but my experience is extremely limited and consists of a ten-minute foray of hands and body parts on an old boyfriend's couch that was in his parents' basement. Not exactly roses and chocolates by a long shot. It hurt, it was over before it got started, and after it was over, he kicked me to the curb, so I gave up.

"You will forget anyone before me," he growls out. "And before I enter you, you will be well-prepared, little mate."

"Let me finish checking her over. I'm sure she'd like to shower and get cleaned up," Doc insists. "You can continue this mental foreplay when I leave."

I can't help the giggle that escapes when Chaos rumbles next to me.

AFTER DOC LEAVES, I REALIZE I HAVE A LOT OF questions with no answers. "Chaos?" I ask, looking at him.

"Hmm?"

"Can you explain what's going to happen to me? I mean, you said earlier I'll be able to shift. Will it hurt? When will it happen?"

"I can't answer that, but I know someone who will have the answers. Why don't you go shower and get cleaned up, and I'll make that call, then find us something to eat."

I realize I don't know what time it is, but it's obviously late at night or even early the next morning, based on the fact my stomach is rumbling. Food actually sounds kind of good right now, which astonishes me, because apparently not so long ago, I was near death.

"Who are you going to call?" I query, curious because he seems so knowledgeable. "And what am I going to wear?" I mean, the outfit I wore to the signing is practically shredded on my body, after all.

"My grandmother. As for what you can wear, the brothers brought your suitcase and I put it in the bathroom."

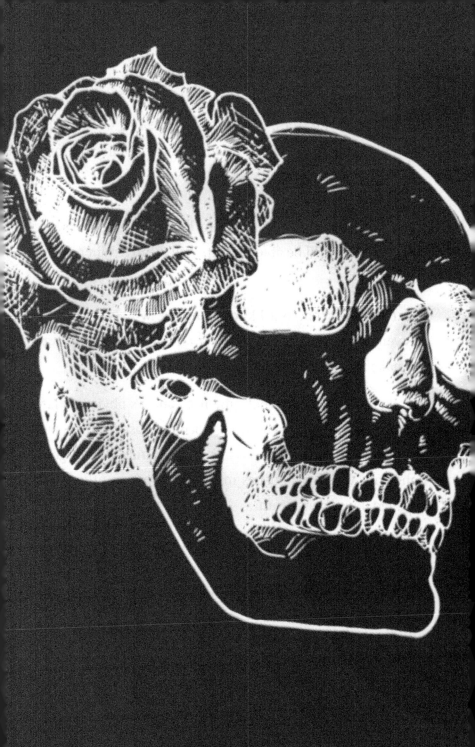

CHAPTER TWELVE

Chaos

After showing her where everything is kept in the bathroom, I leave my room, locking the door behind me, and head down to the kitchen to see what I can get. It's nearly two in the morning, but brothers are still milling around, drinking and partying. Just another typical weekend around here, which has me hastening my steps.

"Chaos!" Fox's voice calls out over the music, and I switch directions to where he's sitting at his usual table. Right now, Renda is underneath, on her knees, so I focus on his face. No need to see his dick for the millionth time. He smirks at me when he notices, taking a pull from his bottle of beer.

DARLENE TALLMAN

"You needed me?" I question, anxious to get back to Tressa once I call my grandmother and find out the answers to her question.

"How's she doing?"

"Not too bad, all things considered," I reply. "It's not every day that you find out something you thought was just a product of an author's mind is, in fact, real. Or that you're going to turn into a wolf yourself." I know my tone is a bit snide, but the adrenaline rush from earlier has worn off, and I'm now bone tired. All I want to do is fix us something to eat, grab a shower, then crash.

He chuckles. "Yeah, I'd say she's doing as good as can be expected. So, Sly and Ogre said her phone's been blowing up. Someone named Nini keeps calling, and has left a shit ton of text messages. Any concerns there?"

"That's her best friend. I suspect we're going to have a visitor sooner rather than later because it sounds like they're close. I don't think my mate has anyone else."

Which makes my cold, dead heart sad on her behalf. I'm surrounded by family, brothers by choice. Plus, while I'm no longer part of my original pack, I have no doubt if I placed a call, they'd show up en masse to help me. She has no one except a friend.

"She does now," Stealth advises, bringing over a couple of beers. Handing me one, he sits down and sucks half of his back in one long swallow. "She's definitely unlike any female we've ever had around here, but I don't think it'll be a bad thing, Brother. Soften our rough edges, so to speak."

"How so?" I bristle a bit at his words, and it comes out in my tone, which has him smirking at me.

"Seriously? Have you seen the inside of her car?" he retorts, chuckling. When I shake my head, he practically snorts beer out of his nose laughing. "Brother, her Jeep is *pink* which is not a standard color. Not only that, but she's got matching floor mats and seat covers. Her purse is all girly too, plus, think about it. She *looks* like she needs to be watched over. You don't think the rest of the brothers won't eat that shit up? Being able to help their brother watch over his defenseless mate? I already overheard one of them yelling at another that once she was up and around, the open sex would have to stop."

I start laughing, doubling over as what he says fully processes. She hasn't even been part of this life for a day, and already my brothers are bending over backwards to ensure she's safe and taken care of. "I'm sure that's gonna piss off a few of them."

"They'll do it or answer to me," Fox decrees, slamming his empty bottle onto the table. He taps Renda's head, and when she pulls off his dick, he shakes his head, shoves himself back into his jeans, then helps her up. "Go grab us some more beers."

I can tell she's a bit stunned; his tone is softer than normal, *and* he helped her get up. Both are total anomalies for him. He's got a reputation for being hard and unyielding, something I've seen firsthand more times than I can count. Is Tressa really going to influence all these fuckers so much?

"Need to grab us some food, we're both hungry, then get some rest. We going to deal with that bastard tomorrow?"

"Tomorrow or the next day, he's not going anywhere, Chaos," Stealth advises, smirking at me. "In fact, he's tied up just like your woman was, and may even have a few matching injuries too. Gives him something to think about while he's cooling his heels."

"Go, get your mate taken care of, Brother," Fox says, waving me away, a gleam in his eyes. "I'm sure there's food in the kitchen."

A few brothers within earshot snicker, but I figure it's because they're buzzed. We don't really get drunk per se; our metabolism is too high, and unless we're chugging liquor, it's more of an enjoyment thing than anything. Shrugging, I place my now empty bottle on the table and head toward the kitchen, only to stop in my tracks when I breach the doorway.

"Nonna?"

"WELL, IF THE MOUNTAIN WON'T COME TO Muhammed, then Muhammed has to come to the mountain," she retorts, stirring something on the stove.

"What are you doing here?"

"Boy, did you seriously expect to find your mate and *not* have me show up?" she asks, putting the spoon down and crossing the room until she's directly in front of me.

Leaning down, I wrap my arms around her in a hug, memories of my past flying through my mind. After she kisses both of my cheeks, she steps back. "Now, to answer your question, I caught it through the family link."

Fuck. Of course, she did, the nosy old bat. Not that I'd ever say that out loud because she'd probably box my ears or something. Nodding, I wait to see what else she has to say.

"So, tell me about her. I was always hopeful you'd find one, but when you left our pack and came here to be part of this lifestyle, I figured it was just wishful thinking."

I grin thinking of Tressa and try to figure out how to explain her to my grandmother. "Well, she's human, for starters, but once I caught her scent, I just knew," I finally say.

"Lilacs or grass?" she questions.

"Both."

Her eyes widen and she mumbles something I can't quite hear before she pulls me over to the table and forces me to sit down. "We need to talk then, because that hasn't happened in more years than I've been alive."

"What do you mean?" I question.

"Most of us, when we find our mates, only catch one of our favorite scents. Legend has it that if you smell two or more, which seems improbable to me, your bond takes on another layer."

What the hell? Why didn't I ever hear this when I was younger? Now, I'm worried about what this means for Tressa.

"What kind of layer?"

"Well, normally our mates are shifters already, not humans, although it *does* happen as you've found out. So, in addition to being able to talk telepathically, and of course, heal the way shifters do, as your bond strengthens, will make you immortal except of course, should you decide to play with barbed wire and get decapitated, or have a bullet fired through your heart."

I slump back in my chair. We age extremely slowly, which is why Tressa has no clue I'm probably double her chronological age, if not more. If what my grandmother is saying is true, we'll be around to see generations of our children grow up.

"Except for losing our heads or having our hearts pierced, I'm sure," I manage to mumble.

"Of course, those are gamechangers, boy. But you'll both heal even faster than usual. Tell me this, what were the circumstances around her coming here?"

I quickly tell her everything outside of club business, and by the time I'm done, her brows are nearly at her hairline. "She hardly has any bruising, or anything left to show from what happened yesterday," I slowly admit, thinking about how she was able to get out of the bed with ease.

"And the two of you haven't even completed the mate bond either," she states. When I glare at her, she snickers. "I'd be willing to bet she's got a lot of questions, am I right?"

"She does, and since I didn't know the answers, I was going to call you, yet you're actually here."

"Let's fix up a tray, then you'll take me to her." It's not a statement, it's a demand as only my Nonna can give. It's something I remember quite well from my younger years, which is why it's hard to beat back the smirk that wants to emerge.

"Yes, Nonna."

What else can I say?

I OPEN THE DOOR AND USHER MY GRANDMOTHER inside. Even though I offered, she rebuffed my attempts to carry the tray, which has me internally chuckling. She's always been a force of nature and it seems that time hasn't changed that aspect of her personality. Once we're inside my room, she moves toward the small table I have in the corner and sets it down while Tressa stands there, shocked and not speaking.

"Little mate, this is my grandmother," I say, walking to where she's standing, holding what looks like the comforter from the bed. "What are you doing?" I ask before looking around and noticing the room now sparkles and the sheets on the bed are fresh.

"What? Oh! Well, after I got cleaned up and dressed, I realized I had laid on the bed with my bloody, dirty clothing, so

I stripped it down then found clean sheets in the cabinet where the towels are at. The only thing is, the comforter needs to be washed since I couldn't find another one of those, and I was going to find a washer and dryer," she says, looking up at me.

My wolf lets out a grumble of approval that our mate is caring for our den, but as I glance at her, I'm stunned.

Why? Because other than a very faint line on her cheek, which is growing fainter the longer I stare at her, both eyes are now open, there's no bruising and her arms, which are mostly bare since she's wearing a T-shirt, show no signs of any of the gashes or cuts she still had, albeit nearly healed, before she went into the shower.

"Holy fuck," I whisper, taking the comforter from her hands. "I'll get one of the prospects to wash this for us." I'm still amazed that she's nearly completely healed considering yesterday afternoon, when I carried her out of that hellhole, she was close to death.

"Chaos!" Nonna snaps. "Language! Come and eat," she instructs, motioning the two of us over to where the food is now artfully placed on the table. Looking at Tressa, she reaches over and pulls her into a hug, which I can tell shocks my mate. "I'm Nonna," she whispers, "and I've been waiting a long time for this one to find his mate."

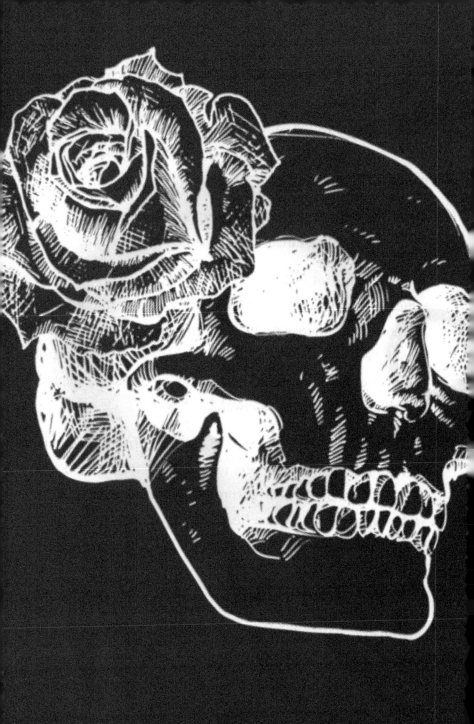

CHAPTER THIRTEEN

TRESSA

I KNOW I'M NOT PARTICULARLY TALL, BUT I STILL manage to dwarf Chaos' grandmother, which is mind boggling. The only people I'm usually taller than are kids as a rule, at least until they hit their growth spurts. Then I'm back to being the short one, well Nini and I are that is, because I'm only a few inches taller than she is! As Nonna leads me over to the table, I catch Chaos smirking before he goes to the door, comforter in hand, and yells for a prospect. A few seconds later, which I consider astonishing, he's closing the door again and walking toward us.

"So, I'm pretty sure you have questions," Nonna states.

"Is that why you're here?" I ask. I'm still trying to wrap my brain around the fact that shifters are real, I'm the fated mate to one, and oh yeah, now I'm going to turn into one myself because he had to bite me to keep me from dropping dead.

Overwhelmed doesn't even begin to cover how my head feels right now. But it's the best word I have for this crazy as hell situation, so I'm going to roll with it.

"Partially, yes," she replies, grinning at Chaos. "This one," she says, pointing at him, "hasn't called home recently so I wanted to make sure he wasn't dead in a ditch because he got his head cut off riding his motorcycle through barbed wire or some shit."

"Nonna, we keep to paved roads," he says. "And not one time in my life, since I started riding, have I ever had the desire to ride my bike through barbed wire. Where you get this shit is anyone's guess."

I can't help the giggle that slips free because he sounds almost... aggrieved? Put out? But even though his tone says one thing, the look on his face is one of patient amusement, so I suspect this is how she is with him.

"I'm glad you don't, especially now that you've found your mate," she retorts before turning and winking at me. "Now, ask me your questions, child."

"Well, what's going to happen? Will it hurt when I shift? *When* will I shift?" I ask, rambling like I normally do.

"Tell me something first. Do you feel any differently inside? Like you're no longer alone in your body?"

I stop and think about what she's asking. While in my shower, I felt like I wasn't alone, like someone was there with me, but not outside the stall. No, it was something else, but I don't think I can describe it.

Slowly nodding my head, I say, "Yes, but I can't explain it in a way that doesn't sound completely crazy."

"It's your wolf, dear. She's making herself at home, and once you've shifted for the first time, you'll be able to feel what she is and know what she's thinking."

"That sounds... interesting," I murmur before shoving some food in my mouth, so I don't babble like a lunatic.

"You're not a lunatic," Chaos whispers, leaning into my side.

"Stop listening to me think!" I exclaim. "What if I go to a weird place in my thoughts? I don't want you regretting this!"

He chuckles while his nonna laughs. "Not gonna happen, little mate. I want to know everything there is to know about you."

"As far as it hurting when you shift. The first few times, it will be uncomfortable as your body gets used to it, but eventually, it'll be like second nature," Nonna states. "As to when, while I'm not one hundred percent positive, I believe it'll be around the time of your next menstrual cycle."

Cue the blush. I can feel my face turning redder than a tomato and focus my gaze on my plate to avoid Chaos' knowing look. Nope, not going there. I mean, I know it's a natural function, but I sure as heck have never talked about my period in front of a guy, and didn't expect to today.

His hand gently strokes my arm as he says, "Nothing to be embarrassed about, Tressa. But you definitely want to figure out when it's set to arrive so we can be prepared for your first shift."

"Some of what I tell you about us, our culture and how things happen, may be different because I'm coming from the perspective of being born a shifter, not being turned. But, once your initial shift happens, the rest of what I tell you should be the same," Nonna announces, casually eating her food as though she didn't just drop a huge bomb on my lap. "Now, finish eating, child. We have much to discuss."

SHE WASN'T WRONG, THAT'S FOR SURE. WHILE CHAOS left to deal with 'club business' which I know from reading my MC books means I'll never know what it's about, Nonna talks about their pack's history and hierarchy, as well as what I can expect with regard to the mate claiming bond, which had me blushing again, and future pregnancies.

At this point, I think I'm permanently red, but I'm also fascinated. She told me his room has never been breached by a woman until today, as his wolf considers it his den and those are strictly for their mate. Outside of one of the girls coming in to clean, his bed has been slept in only by him. Now, I'm down in the kitchen with her as we prepare food for everyone, with help from the three club girls who live here.

"Do you think Chaos will let you come with us on our next spa day?" Teeny asks as she chops tomatoes.

"Um, I don't know, but I can always ask," I reply, pulling another potato toward me so I can peel it. As shifters, we apparently eat a lot of meat, but sides are important too as Nonna said.

"If you need anything, just let us know," Becca says from the sink where she's washing the dishes we've already used.

Nonna is standing at the main table, smiling, while seasoning the meat that's going to be put on the grill at some point. She occasionally adds a comment here and there, but for the most part, I think she's just observing my interaction with the club girls.

"Can I just say something?" I blurt out, which has four sets of eyes now trained on me. "Um, well, I know what I read is fiction, but in most of those books, the club girls are not this nice when one of the men claims a woman as his old lady, or in this case, his mate."

Peals of laughter echo in the vast kitchen space as I try to keep from being embarrassed. But one of the things Nini taught me is that if I don't know something, I should ask, which is what I did.

"Okay, so one thing you'll learn about wolves is they're not particularly monogamous until they find their mate. What we do for the club? While it would be looked at with a lot of side eye in the human world, it isn't in ours. Wolves are sexual creatures, Tressa, so while we know Chaos is off the menu now because of you, at the same time, we're very happy for him because at the end of the day, we all want a mate," Renda finally supplies once she has her laughter in check.

I'm not sure how I feel knowing all three have had sex with Chaos, despite the fact that up until two days ago, I didn't even know he existed. Teeny must see something on my face because she stops what she's doing and comes over to put her arm on my shoulder.

"You don't have to worry about us, Tressa. He never really fucked us, he would only let us give him blowjobs and even then, it wasn't all that often. I think he was holding out for his mate," she softly says.

Great, like I'm oh-so-experienced in *that* area! Sighing, I put my hand up in the universal stop gesture. "It's okay. I mean if you did have sex with him, I can't be upset because I wasn't on his radar. But I don't want to know, okay? I promise, I won't think less of any of you if you took care of him in that way." I know my face is beyond flaming crimson at this point, but I like these girls and feel like maybe we can be friends, so whatever I have to do to ensure it's not awkward between us, that's what I'm going to do.

"Enough chatter, children, let's get this finished," Nonna decrees, thankfully changing the subject. "Now, what should we make for dessert?"

DINNER IS UNLIKE ANYTHING I'VE EVER experienced before in my entire life. First of all, the men of the club can eat; I anticipated that there would be leftovers, but they managed to demolish all five platters of meat. The sides were also heavily dented, but I think us women did more damage there. For dessert, we ended up making one of Chaos' favorites, banana pudding, and after claiming one container for himself, he begrudgingly relented, and allowed the rest of us to get some.

He's been very attentive toward me as well, bringing me a plate piled high with the most succulent pieces of meat, as well as an array of the salads and sides we made earlier. A girl could definitely get used to being taken care of, that's for sure.

Now, we're back in his room and I feel awkward once again. I'm taking another shower, unable to get clean enough from my experience, and wondering how tonight's going to play out, when it dawns on me that I haven't called Nini.

"Dang it, she's going to be so worried!" I mumble, quickly finishing my shower, then drying off and getting into my pajamas. Thankfully, I piled my hair up on my head, so I don't have to go through the hassle of drying it again. Tossing my dirty clothes in the hamper that has miraculously appeared, I head back into the room to see Chaos reclining on the bed, his head wet from his own shower.

Not that he showered with me, darn it all. But I'm not ready for that yet, so I push that thought far, far away. He smirks at me as I round the bed to my side, and I know he caught some of what I was thinking. Again.

Once I'm in bed, I glance at him and ask, "Did... did your brothers find my phone by any chance?"

"They did, along with your purse. Your Jeep is parked in the back of the clubhouse where we put the cages."

Ha! At least I know what *that* means so I don't have to ask another crazy question.

"I need to call Nini," I tell him.

"That's probably a good idea, little one, because she's been blowing up your phone. I've got it charging right now, and it's late, so how about you call her in the morning?

"Doesn't look like I've got much choice. She's never going to believe half of this! Wait, am I allowed to tell her I'm a shifter now? And... will I be staying here?"

"You're with me," he growls. "As far as telling her, let's see how that plays out. I know we don't typically tell humans, but you two seem very close so you probably don't have secrets from one another."

"We don't as a rule, but if I'm not allowed to, I guess I'll deal," I mumble, pouting.

"Come, little mate, you may be fully healed, but you've had a busy twenty-four hours, let's get some rest."

"Okay."

Despite never having slept with another person in my bed before, when he curls around me and throws his arm over my waist, I feel a sense of safety and security I've never had before.

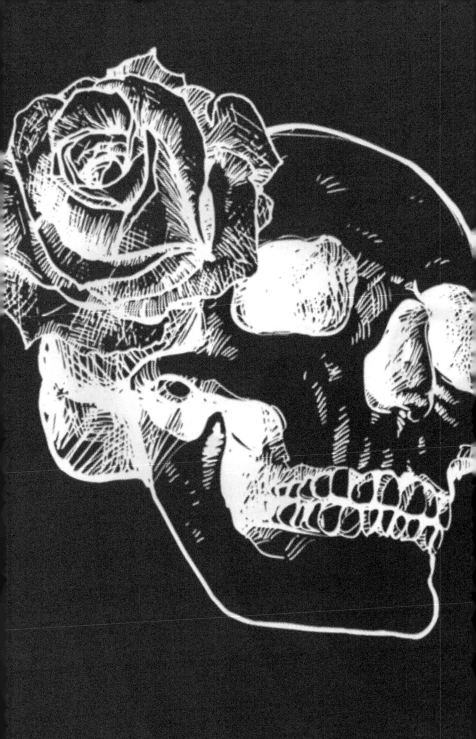

CHAPTER FOURTEEN

Chaos

Sleeping next to my mate just might be the death of me. As she slumbers, I lay there trying not to give in to the need to fully claim her. *Patience, asshole,* I tell myself. *All of this is new to her.* Despite the fact I physically want her, the contentment that seeps into my body at the fact my mate is in my arms lulls me into a deep slumber.

"Little mate, what are you doing?" I mumble, trying to open my eyes.

"I'm so hot, Chaos," she whispers, her hands roaming over my body. In deference to her, I put on a pair of cut-off sweats but normally, I'm naked because shifters tend to be hot-natured.

"I'm not surprised," I tell her, taking a good look at what she's wearing. "Didn't Nonna tell you we tend to run hotter than a human?"

"She did but I guess I didn't fully understand." I hear her gasp, then she says, "Holy smokes, even though it's dark in here, I can see you clearly!"

"Because of your wolf, Tressa," I patiently reply. "Hold on, let me get you something lighter to wear."

Rolling out of my bed, I walk over to my dresser and pull the top drawer open, grabbing a T-shirt that I know will probably be too big on her, but it'll be a lot cooler for her to wear than the two-piece pajama set she currently has on. Handing it to her, I'm totally unprepared for her to practically shred her pajamas before she slides the shirt over her head, audibly sighing.

Her body, which would normally be barely discernible in the darkened room to a human, is exquisite. Full, rosy-tipped breasts that beg to be fondled; a narrow waist that flares out into hips perfect for carrying our future pups. I can feel my own body responding, especially when I catch a whiff of her own arousal and see her face flush.

"Are you okay, little one?" I cautiously ask, when instead of going back to bed, she takes a hesitant step in my direction.

"I... I think so," she murmurs. "It just dawned on me, Chaos, that you haven't kissed me."

I can't help the smirk that crosses my lips at her words. Right now, she's equal parts temptress and innocent, and both are calling to my soul in a way I never dreamed would be possible. "So, before you can sleep, I should kiss you, hmm?" I ask once she's right in front of me.

"Yes," she teases, smiling up at me. "I mean, your grandmother explained how it is with mates, but what if we don't have any chemistry? That would suck."

The chuckle that bursts free has her blush deepening so I reach out to pull her into my arms. "Didn't mean to embarrass you, little mate. The gods don't make mistakes when it comes to mates, so the last thing you need to worry about is whether or not we'll be compatible. Now, you mentioned me kissing you?"

Her nod is quick which pleases both me and my wolf. We *want* her eager to spend time with us, to touch us, to kiss us. Wolves are typically very sensual creatures, and while it's been extremely difficult to keep from enjoying what the club girls could give me, I knew it would be a temporary fix, so I elected to hold off. The brief times I gave in and let them suck me off were merely because I couldn't handle another run in the woods, or taking another shower to rub one out while thoughts of my possible mate ran like a movie in my head.

As she wraps her arms over my shoulders, I lower my head and breathe in her fragrance, which is now surrounding us. Heady delight swarms me when our lips lightly touch, especially when her breath hitches at the contact and she moves closer.

Long moments pass as I memorize her taste before gliding my tongue along her lower lip. When she opens, I finally gain entry and soon, we're both moaning. Breathless, I pull back slightly and lean my forehead against hers.

"Definitely getting hot in here," I murmur, chuckling. I can feel her hardened nipples brushing against my bare chest, and whether she's aware of it or not, she's been lightly grinding against my rock-hard cock since our lips first touched.

"Just a little," she agrees.

"C'mon, little one, let's get back in bed so we're comfortable," I suggest, leading her to my side where I watch with heated eyes as she crawls in then flops down on her side so she's facing me.

Copying her position, I rest with my head on my arm so I'm looking at her. I can see her wolf peering out at me and feel my own wolf respond in kind, rumbling his excitement in my chest. As I brush her hair back with my hand, she sighs in contentment, leaning in for my caress. Even though I'm worried she's not ready for what I want to do, she's definitely sending all the signals, so I decide to take the bull by the horns and ask, which isn't normally my style.

Except... with her, I want to be sure she knows what us having sex will mean. Wolves mate for life; there is no leaving, no separation, and no timeouts. Only death will ever part us, and based on what Nonna said earlier, that won't happen for a very long time. Add to it the fact she's also now my old lady, and quite frankly, she's stuck with me. Of course, I plan to marry her at some point as well, once her human mind catches up with her wolf's instincts to mate.

"Chaos?" she asks, breaking into my reverie.

"Hmm?" I hum.

"Will you... will you make love to me?"

TIME STOPS AS I LOOK AT HER TO SEE SHE'S FLUSHED, but it's from arousal, not embarrassment. She meets my gaze head on, keeping my stare and igniting my body, not once looking away as I peruse her no matter how heated my thoughts become.

"Are you sure, little mate? We don't have to just yet, you went through a pretty traumatic experience after all." My natural instinct is to pounce, bite, and claim her. But what kind of mate would I be if I didn't put her best interest first? Because as far as I'm concerned, her well-being will always be my utmost priority.

My wolf powerfully slams himself into my chest, causing me to grunt, because he's not happy with me trying to hold her off. What he doesn't grasp is she had to be absolutely terrified by the things they said to her; the last thing I want is anything we do to cause her any fear or anxiety. After I communicate that to him, he huffs then slinks over to the corner of my mind and slumps down, whining.

"Which I'm completely healed from," she counters. If she were standing up, I just know she'd have her hands on her hips, that's how confident she sounds right now. "Please?"

Deciding she knows herself better than I do at this point, I roll so she's partially under me, and begin kissing her once again.

CHAPTER FIFTEEN

TRESSA

I'M UNSURE WHERE MY BOLDNESS IS COMING FROM, but I suspect it's my wolf taking charge and making herself known. All I know is that I want this man more than I've ever wanted anything in my life. I don't want to wait, I want to be fully his in every way I can be. As his kisses grow bolder, I find myself moaning, my body lighting up as though I'm a piece of kindling that's been struck with a match. Everywhere he touches, fiery pleasure starts to pulse until I'm a ball of needy, begging mess.

When he leans back, I reach down and pull his T-shirt over my head, leaving me bare, except for the panties I left on when I tore off my pajamas earlier. I see his gaze roam over my body and briefly wonder if he's happy with how I look.

"Ecstatic comes to mind," he growls out, his hand coming up to cup my breast. As his thumb teases my already taut nipple, I reach out to stroke my fingers across his chest. He's got chest hair, more than a dusting, and I can't wait to feel it against me, brushing against my skin.

"Really?"

I don't want to bring anyone into our bed, but those old insecurities are trying to rear their ugly heads, so I can't help the question that slips from my lips—it's better to know than to let troubling thoughts ruin the moment and mess with my head. He raises one brow but doesn't answer; instead, he leans in and takes my turgid nipple between his lips.

Holy guacamole, Batman! I think there's an invisible link between my nip and my clit if the dampness that's flooded my nether region is any indication. At the rate I'm going, I'll have an orgasm before we ever get to the good stuff, which would be mortifying. Granted, I've never had one during sex before, so there's that small worry to consider, but I suspect he knows what he's doing, so I'm going to relax and enjoy the ride so to speak.

When he lightly nips me before switching sides, I squeal, which elicits a chuckle from him. "Just don't want you getting lost in your head, Tressa," he teases.

"Nope, not me. I'm one hundred percent right here," I breathlessly blather.

"You have nothing to worry about, mate. I'll be well-pleased with you," he informs me before sucking, licking, and nipping my other breast and nipple until I'm writhing against him trying to ease the throbbing that's now going on between my legs.

He eases down the bed, taking my underwear with him and tossing it to the side before he settles between my thighs, and just breathes me in. When I try to close my thighs, he uses his large hands to push them apart, then he places them in a position so his fingers are lightly stroking the inside of my legs as he slowly slides his tongue through my folds.

"Chaos," I breathe out on a sigh. I know I've read more sex scenes than I can remember, but I always thought the author took creative license when it came to how their heroine felt when the hero went down on her, like most artists tend to do when working their craft. In short, I thought they were embellishing the whole thing because after all, they were writing fiction, right?

They weren't.

Not by a longshot.

As his more than capable tongue and lips work me into a fevered pitch, he slides one finger inside, causing me to moan out in pleasure.

"Fuck, little one, you're tight. Gonna feel fucking phenomenal when I have your wet pussy wrapped around my dick," he murmurs against me. "But first, you're going to come on my tongue and fingers," he commands.

Pulses of pleasure rush through me at his continued onslaught and I realize I'm about to experience something I've only felt by my own hand. *Except this time, it's going to be huge, unlike anything I've known before.*

"Chaos," I keen out, my back arching off the bed as I shoot into the stratosphere. By the time I come down from my orgasmic high, he's naked, and I can feel the head of his cock notched at my entrance.

"Look at us, Tressa," he insists. "See how well you take my dick into your wet, warm sheath."

Mesmerized, I watch as he slowly enters me, inch by agonizing inch, my pussy gripping him tightly as he works his way in until he's seated against my mound. When he slowly pulls back, then thrusts inside again, I moan, my head falling back as my hands grip his shoulders. He sets a steady rhythm, swiveling his hips in such a way that he hits my clit every time he bottoms out.

I wrap my legs around his waist, my hips now rising to meet him, and soon, his momentum morphs into a quicker pace as our breathing becomes choppy and erratic. I can feel my pussy start to flutter and realize I'm about to come again, something I didn't think I was capable of doing. Hell, again, I was positive multiple orgasms were mythical, like unicorns, and maybe for some, they are, but that's definitely not going to be an issue where we're concerned!

"Chaos," I warn.

"Let it go, little mate, it'll make it easier when I bite you," he encourages, leaning in to lick at the juncture between my shoulder and neck.

Trusting him, I focus on how he's making my body feel, and when his thumb strokes over my clit, I detonate, screaming his name just as I feel his teeth puncture my skin. A flash of pain, followed by rampant ecstasy, courses through me as I feel him thrust several more times then stop and suddenly warmth fills me as he finds his own release.

Limp and satiated, I feel like purring as he licks the bite then rolls so I'm sprawled over him before he pulls the covers back over us. "That was phenomenal," I murmur, already sliding into sleep, finally worn completely out.

"Yes, it was," he murmurs, gently kissing me. "Sleep, little mate. I've got you."

———

I DON'T KNOW HOW LONG I'VE BEEN SLEEPING, BUT when I wake up, I realize something's not right when I try to speak and hear a short yip instead. What the heck? Looking down, I see paws, not my arms or legs, and fear courses through me. Nonna said it would happen closer to when I was going to start my period and that's not for a few weeks! Nudging Chaos, I wait for him to wake up, and when he does, his eyes grow huge.

"Fuck. Let me go get Nonna," he says, rolling out of the bed. "On second thought, do you want to go run?"

I yip again, turning on the bed a few times to show I'm excited.

"Can you understand me, Tressa?" he asks.

"Yes! I just don't understand why it happened like this. Can we get her, then run?" I question.

He slips on his sweats as I jump off the bed, wagging my tail as I follow him from the room. The party is apparently still going on downstairs, and we garner quite a few looks when we walk through the common room.

"Someone grab my nonna," Chaos hollers. "We're going to run so she can see what it's like."

He leads us to the back porch where we find his nonna sitting in one of the chairs, a serene smile on her face. "I've been waiting for you two," she says.

"Nonna, you told her it would happen differently," Chaos accuses. "She woke up like this!"

"After you gave her the claiming mark, right, boy?" she questions, smirking at him. I'm surprised to see him flush before he nods. "I told you also that with you smelling two scents, things were different. Remember, child, that this hasn't happened in several generations, so all I have to go on is the lore. Now, Tressa, let me look at you."

I bound over to her then sit, my head tilted and tongue lolling out. I'm feeling all kinds of things right now; all the smells in the air surrounding me are driving me crazy and I want to chase after them. The funny thing is, I smell snickerdoodle cookies, which are my favorite cookies in the world right now, and that's impossible.

Maybe I really *did* die, and this is all a dream? The smell of cookies is a brain bleed or something?

"You didn't die, child. If you're smelling something that's not normally outside, it means you have your mate's scent now. I wasn't sure if you'd get it or not since you were turned, but it seems as though you did," Nonna states. "You're beautiful, isn't she, Chaos?" she questions, looking over at my mate, who looks like he's been struck by a two-by-four.

He crouches next to me, and I feel his hands running through my fur, eliciting a happy yip, followed by my tongue swiping across his cheek, which makes him laugh. "Yes, she is," he replies, looking at me. "Nonna, we're going to run, can you let the boys know they're welcome to come and join us, so she understands what it's like to run as a pack with our family?"

"I've got it, child," she says. "Now, go play with your mate."

I DON'T KNOW HOW LONG WE RUN, BUT THE REST OF his brothers, as well as the club girls, eventually join us, and I learn what it means to play in this form. Gone is my shyness, my insecurity about not being enough, my worry over what someone else thinks of me. Instead, I feel confident, brave, and strong.

The sun is about to rise when we make our way back to the porch. I'm exhausted, but as I see everyone else shift then grab their clothes to head inside and probably to bed, I realize there's no way I can handle being naked in front of a bunch of strangers. When Chaos looks at me, I whine, forgetting we can talk without speaking.

"What's the matter, little mate? Are you afraid to shift back?" he asks. I shake my head. *"Or are you worried about everyone seeing you naked?"* I nod while barking. *"Okay, then, I get it, Tressa. This is new for you, and my wolf isn't thrilled about my brothers seeing you naked either, so follow me, okay?"*

I follow him to our room, no, our *den*, exhausted but happy that I seemed to hold my own during all the rough and tumble games we played with the others.

CHAPTER SIXTEEN

CHAOS

WAKING UP TO FIND TRESSA HAD SHIFTED WHILE WE slept was a bit unsettling. I'm sure my nonna will be reaching out to older members of my family pack to see what other anomalies our mating may bring about, but right now, as she walks alongside me, I feel pride rising up in my chest.

Despite everything that's been thrown at her in the past two days, she's been nothing but a trooper. I just hope she doesn't struggle when shifting back. Guess I'll deal with it if it happens, but most likely, she'll breeze through that as well.

Once we're inside our den, and the door is locked, I crouch so we're eye level and say, "Okay, to shift back, just picture yourself as a human. I'm right here and will help if you need me to." While I may not be the 'alpha' of this particular pack of people, my lineage has given me the ability to tap into those powers if needed so I can help her shift should she run into any problems.

She nods her head and then closes her eyes, which makes me smile a bit. I think I've smiled and laughed more since meeting her than I have my entire life, and anticipate a lifetime of joy that only she's able to give me.

"Whoa, that was... that was freaking awesome!" she says, sitting there naked on her haunches. "And it didn't hurt!"

I pull her up and into my arms, kissing her soundly. "Now, for my favorite part after a run," I tease, scooping her up bridal style.

"What's that?" she asks, her voice now breathless.

"A nice hot shower," I reply, walking into the bathroom.

I set her on her feet then turn the water on, adjusting the temperature until it's just right. Helping her in, I grin seeing the mate mark at her shoulder. When she moans at the feel of the water hitting her back, my dick takes notice, causing me to chuckle. "How do you feel about shower sex?" I question, moving closer to her.

"I... I don't know," she says, looking up at me with heated eyes.

"Let's find out, shall we?"

"WELL, THAT WAS FUN," SHE DROWSILY MURMURS, draped over my body as I settle us into bed. "Can we do that every time after a run?"

"As often as you'd like," I reply, kissing her. "Now rest. I'm sure you're going to want to call your friend when we wake up."

"God, yes. That is, if she's not already halfway here."

"OH, HELL. UM, CHAOS?"

I suspect there's a learning curve with having a mate and what I'm seeing for me is interrupted sleep. Opening one eye, I see Tressa sitting up in bed, her phone in her hand. She waves it at me and to give credit where it's due, I can't see a damn thing right now, but I suspect there are missed calls and texts from her friend.

"What, little mate?" I ask, my voice raspy with sleep.

"Look at these!" she exclaims, shoving the phone in my hand.

> Nini: Tress, you haven't called me yet. Does that mean the date is going well?

> Nini: Okay, wench, it's been two hours since my last text and you still haven't called or responded. Hell, you haven't even read it yet. Are you okay?

> Nini: Tressa, answer me, dammit! I'm officially worried now that it's been FOUR HOURS!

> Nini: If you don't answer me, I'm going to presume you're dead in a ditch and start calling hospitals.

> Nini: Okay, this isn't funny anymore. I've called all the hospitals in the area and you're not there, no one has seen you since mid-afternoon at the event venue, and I'm officially beyond pissed and now worried. ANSWER ME!

> Nini: I KNEW Life 360 would be a godsend. I am on my way, and someone better have answers as to what the fuck is going on.

Glancing at her I grin. "Sounds like she's on her way," I tease.

"You have no idea what Hurricane Nicole can do," she retorts. "You better warn your brothers because she's not afraid to catch a charge if she thinks I've been hurt."

A knock on the door has me knifing up and answering it, not bothering to put any clothes on. It's not like we haven't all seen each other naked, so why bother?

"Um, Brother?" Ogre asks. "Think you and your mate need to get downstairs. All hell is breaking loose right now. Her friend is down there and giving Stealth absolute hell."

AFTER QUICKLY DONNING CLOTHES, WE RACE downstairs to see a woman, who I presume is Tressa's best friend, in a sort of standoff with Stealth and Sly. She has one hand on her hip and the other is inside her purse as though she's got a gun or another weapon. Not that anything short of a machete to the neck or a direct hit to the heart would be more than an inconvenience, but still, it's a bit nerve wracking to see my brothers backing down from the petite brunette.

"And I'm telling you right fucking now, Life 360 says she's here, and I'm not leaving until I see her! I don't care who I have to mow down, do you understand me?" the curvy brunette yells. When Stealth tries to get closer, she gives him a scathing look and shakes her purse in a threatening manner. He throws his hands up in a conciliatory way and slowly backs up to stand where he originally started.

"Nini?" Tressa calls out. "It's okay, I'm right here. I'm sorry I didn't call or text, but things got a little...chaotic... then my phone died. Chaos put it on the charger, and I just saw the messages."

Nini whirls and nearly plows my mate down when she reaches her, wrapping her arms around her, and shaking her back and forth as tears flow down her cheeks. "Dead in a ditch is what I suspected until I remembered we put that stupid app on our phones," she murmurs. "What the hell happened?"

"It's a long story," Tressa replies before her eyes grow wide when Stealth snatches Nini's purse and dumps it over onto a nearby table.

Oh fuck. If the fire I see in Nini's eyes is any indication, Stealth's about to fry.

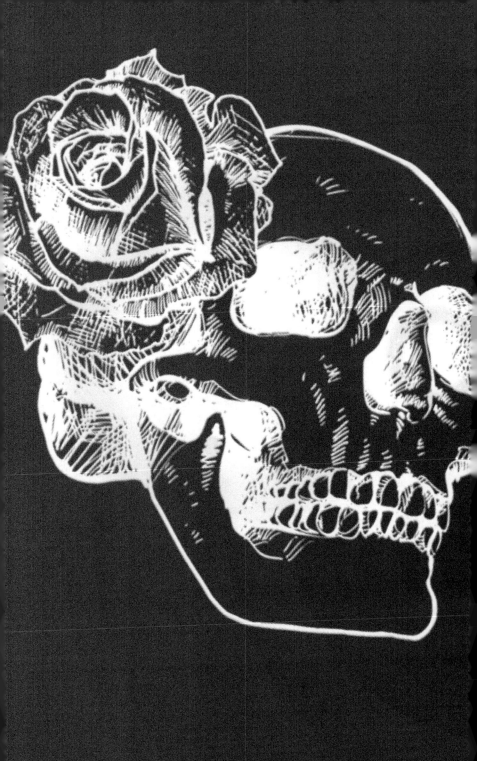

CHAPTER SEVENTEEN

TRESSA

"WHAT IS HE DOING?" I WHISPER-YELL AT CHAOS. "Does he not know *anything* about women? You do not touch their purses!"

"Noted, little one," he murmurs against my ear.

Now, I'm fearful for Chaos' brother's life as Nini turns on Stealth and proceeds to whack him in the chest. Not because I think she can hurt him per se, but because he looks like he's been struck by a train.

"Woman, what the fuck is all this shit?" Stealth asks, looking down at Nini.

"It's not shit, *caveman*, it's my stuff," Nini sneers, making me hide my grin behind my hand.

Nini's beyond organized; she has a place for everything, and everything has a place. Except for her purse. She always starts out with great intentions, vowing that only her wallet, a couple of pens, her period pouch, and an emergency makeup and meds bag will reside in her purse. Then, a few weeks later, she's tossing in change, extra straws and napkins, receipts, small notebooks, and hair ties. The cycle has repeated itself so many times since we became friends, that I'm used to it by now, but Stealth looks shocked at all the stuff littering the top of the table from her overturned purse.

"What is this?" he questions, picking up what looks like a chocolate dick. The giggle that bursts free has Nini glaring at me before she smiles.

"Oh! I figured we could put some of Tressa's business cards on it and hand them out at any of the signings we go to as readers," she enthuses.

"A chocolate cock?" Ogre asks, before bursting into laughter. "It looks like it came too, based on the white icing, or what-ever it is, coming from the tip."

His comment has me flushing while all the brothers chuckle. While Chaos isn't doing it out loud, I can feel his body vibrating against mine since he pulled me into his chest and has his arms wrapped around me right now.

"You carry chocolate dicks around?" Stealth growls out, looking at Nini like he wants to shake her. "What kind of business would use those?"

"*Authors*, dumbass. She makes covers and edits for romance authors, and surprise, surprise, they write about S-E-X, you Neanderthal. Thus, chocolate dicks!" Nini spreads her hands wide, and I half expect her to yell out, "Superstar!" like that stupid ass movie, which still makes us both laugh, especially when we've had some wine.

"My mate will *not* be handing out chocolate dicks to anyone," Chaos growls out. When I look up at him, I see his wolf peering at me and know we'll have to find something else catchy, although, I'm sure it would've gotten a lot of attention.

"What's with all the receipts?" Ogre adds, trying to rifle through the detritus that is Nini's purse. Only, he never gets the chance because Stealth smacks him.

Hmm. Interesting. I also catch the man in question leaning toward Nini, *my* Nini, and before I can help it, I growl out a warning. No one messes with her, not on my watch! I gasp when I realize what I've done, especially when Nini turns in my direction and asks, "Why did I hear a dog growling just now?"

Before I can answer, Nonna steps forward and looks at everyone standing around. Clearing her throat, I see her give Chaos a pointed look, and when he sighs before nodding, she starts to speak. "It wasn't a dog, child. It was a wolf. Tressa's wolf, to be precise. She didn't particularly care for the fact that Stealth was moving so close to you."

Nini's eyes grow wide, like cartoons show sometimes when a character is shocked, as she stares at me. "Wolf? *Tressa's* wolf? What on earth is going on?"

She looks almost scared now as she eyes all the men, who are tall, as well as heavily muscled, and I move away from Chaos to comfort her. "Nini, remember how we read that one series and thought how awesome it would be if shifters were real?" At her nod, I smile and continue. "Well, guess what, they are!"

"No way. No fucking way. I knew that sweet tea I got at my last stop tasted funny. I'm obviously hallucinating, and you're just being mean teasing me like this," she stammers, her face turning crimson red.

"I'm not teasing you, Nini, I promise," I softly reply. I'm not skilled enough to do what Chaos is able to do, so instead, I concentrate on bringing forth my wolf, and am soon looking up at my best friend, who is so stunned she nearly falls backward, until Stealth's arms grab her and place her in a chair.

"Tressa?" she whispers, staring at me. I sit back on my haunches and give her what I hope is a grin, but probably looks more like a deranged grimace. What can I say? I'm still learning about all of this as well. "Holy shit. Are... are all of you able to do that?" she asks, looking around once again. When all the guys nod, she appears as though she's going to faint, so I nuzzle her hand. "This is beyond anything I expected when I encouraged you to go to that signing, Tress!"

I yip several times because laughing in this form isn't possible, and since I shifted, I refuse to shift back. There's no way I want to stand here naked in front of all of Chaos' brothers. Nope. Not me.

"Won't happen, little mate," he advises in a soothing voice. *"Once we get her settled, you can go back to our den and shift. I'm sure you two have a lot to discuss."*

"WELL, I TAKE IT YOU'RE STAYING HERE," SHE SAYS AS we sit at a table away from everyone else. She's been talking quietly, but I know all of the men have been subtly listening in as she asks question after question.

I shudder because the thought of *not* being by Chaos' side is abhorrent to me. "Yeah, Nini. He's my mate, and these are his brothers, his family. But you're my family, too."

"It might take me a month or two, but I'll get our place all packed up and move out here. See, problem solved," she replies, grinning at me. "Shouldn't be too hard to find another job, right?"

"I wouldn't think so," I say, grinning back. "Of course, we can't tell *anyone*. The only reason Nonna told you is because Chaos gave her the go-ahead to do so."

"Huh. Okay, so, is there anything you don't mind parting with?" she asks, pulling a pen and one of her little note-books out of her purse, which has been put back together once again.

I stop and think about what she's asking me. I have my laptop, as well as the rest of my electronics and their respective chargers already. But I'll need my desktop, my desk, the rest of my clothes, and the knick-knacks I've acquired during the years we've lived together.

"I guess my bedroom furniture, that kind of thing. Should I come back with you to help? I mean, I have my fireproof box with all my important papers I'll need, but the bank I use has a branch here, so there are no worries on that end. What do you think?"

"If she needs to come out to help, we'll get her there," Chaos promises, walking up and placing two frozen margaritas on the table. Leaning in, he kisses me, then heads back over to the pool tables.

"Okay, I guess that answers that question, huh?" she teases, before jotting down a few notes.

"How long can you stay? Maybe we can find you a place to rent before you go back home?" I ask.

"I'll have to head out tomorrow because I have to work in a few days. Need to get the ball rolling as far as giving notice and all that crap," she replies, writing something else done. "I still can't believe they're real," she murmurs, causing me to grin.

"Everything we've read is so on target, too," I enthuse, wiggling my brows at her, which causes her to giggle. I hear a grunt and look over to see Stealth scowling in our direction as Chaos laughs. Guess he missed his shot or something.

"What a great adventure you've had," she finally says, putting the pen and paper away so she can focus on her drink.

"Well, some of it wasn't all that great," I reply, my eyes narrowing as I think of my kidnapping and near-death experience. "But, in the end, it all worked out so there's that, right?"

"I can't wait to see what the future holds once I get here!" she exclaims.

Raising my glass, I tap it against hers and reply, "Here's to happily ever after and all that jazz."

THE END...OF CHAOS AND TRESSA'S STORY...

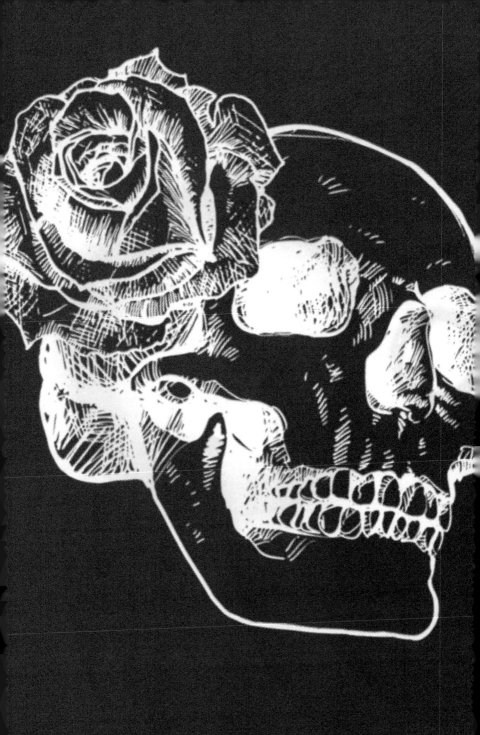

EPILOGUE

STEALTH

EVER SINCE THE BRUNETTE DYNAMO CAME WALTZING into the clubhouse and I caught her scent, I've been off kilter. What are the fucking odds that *my* mate would be best friends with Chaos' woman? If you had asked me before all this, I would have said slim to none.

Yet, as I watch her pull out of the parking lot, giving Tressa a jaunty wave while somehow managing to beep her horn, I feel my fists clenching in dismay. My wolf is trying to claw me from the inside out, livid because we, no *I*, allowed her to drive away.

As if I had any say in the matter. Outside of when she was yelling at me the day she first arrived, she stuck by Tressa's side as they made lists covering every possible scenario with regard to her moving here.

Once I'm sure she's out of sight, I throw back my head and howl out my anguish. Time to run.

AUTHOR'S NOTE - THE SAA WILL BE BOOK TWO IN THE ZEPHYR HILLS MC SERIES, AND WILL BE AVAILABLE SOMETIME THIS YEAR!

ABOUT THE AUTHOR

I am a transplanted Yankee, moving from upstate New York when I was a teenager. I'm a mom of four and grandma of nine who has found a love of traveling that I never knew existed! I live with the brat-cat pack (all rescues) as well as my dog, Bosco, 'deep in the heart of Texas', as I plot and plan who will get to "talk" next!

Find me on Facebook!

https://www.facebook.com/darlenetallmanauthor

Darlene's Dolls (my reader's group): https://www.facebook.com/groups/1024089434417791/permalink/1063976267095774/?comment_id=1063979757095425&notif_id=1539553456785632&notif_t=group_comment

DARLENE'S BOOKS

The Black Tuxedos MC

1. The Black Tuxedos MC - Reese
2. Nick - The Black Tuxedos MC
3. Matt - The Black Tuxedos MC

Poseidon's Warriors MC

1. Poseidon's Lady
2. Trident's Queen
3. Loki's Angel
4. Brooks' Bride
5. Atlas' World
6. The Warriors' Hearts (novella)
7. Kaya's King

8. Chelsea's Knight
9. Orion's Universe

Zephyr Hills MC (Mayhem Makers)

The Enforcer
The SAA (2023 release TBD)

Writing in the Rogue Enforcers World

Paxton: A Rogue Enforcers Novel
Esmerelda: A Rogue Enforcers Novel
Charisma: A Rogue Enforcers Novella (with Liberty Parker)

Writing in the Royal Bastards MC world (Roanoke, VA chapter)

Brick's House
A Very Merry Brick-mas
Banshee's Lament - releases June 2023

Standalones

Bountiful Harvest
His Firefly
His Christmas Pixie
Her Kinsman-Redeemer

Operation Valentine

His Forever

Forgiveness

Christmas With Dixie

Our Last First Kiss

Draegon: The Falder Clan - Book One

Scars of the Soul

Hale's Song

Mountain Ink: Mountain Mermaids Sapphire Lake

Knox's Jewel: A Dark Leopards MC Novella

Desire: A Savage Wilde Novel

Contraryed: A Heels, Rhymes & Nursery Crimes short
story

Sashy's Salvation

Search & Find

Little Red's

Rebel Guardians MC (with Liberty Parker)

1. Braxton

2. Hatchet

3. Chief

4. Smokey & Bandit

5. Law

6. Capone

7. A Twisted Kind of Love

Rebel Guardians Next Generation (with Liberty Parker)

1. Talon & Claree
2. Jaxson & Ralynn
3. Maxum & Lily

New Beginnings (with Liberty Parker)

1. Reclaiming Maysen
2. Reviving Luca
3. Restoring Tig

Where Are They Now? RGMC updates on original 7 couples (with Liberty Parker)
Braxton
Hatchet
Chief

Nelson Brothers (with Liberty Parker)

1. Seeking Our Revenge
2. Seeking Our Forever
3. Seeking Our Destiny

Rebellious Christmas (A Christmas Novella) (with Liberty Parker)

Nelson Brothers Ghost Team Series (with Liberty Parker)

1. Alpha
2. Bravo

Old Ladies Club (with Kayce Kyle, Erin Osborne and Liberty Parker)

1. Old Ladies Club - Wild Kings MC
2. The Old Ladies Club - Soul Shifterz MC
3. Old Ladies Club - Rebel Guardians MC
4. Old Ladies Club - Rage Ryders MC

The Mischief Kitties (with Cherry Shephard)

The Mischief Kitties in Bampires & Ghosts & New Friends, Oh My!
The Mischief Kitties in the Great Glitter Caper
The Mischief Kitties in You Can't Takes Our Chicken

Raven Hills Coven (with Liberty Parker)

1. Rise of the Raven
2. Whimsical
3. Enchantment
4. Prophecy Revealed

Tattered and Torn MC (with Erin Osborne)

1. Letters from Home/War (novella)
2. Letters Between Us (novella)
3. Letters of Healing (novella)
4. Letters from Mom (novella)
5. Letters to Heaven (novella)
6. Letters with Love (novella)
7. Letters from Nanny (novella)
8. Letters of Wisdom (novella)
9. Band of Letters - all 8 novellas in one volume
10. Her Keeper
11. Her One
12. Her Absolution

Made in the USA
Middletown, DE
02 September 2024